Love is
a time of enchantment:
in it all days are fair and all fields
green. Youth is blest by it,
old age made benign:
the eyes of love see
roses blooming in December,
and sunshine through rain. Verily
is the time of true-love
a time of enchantment — and
Oh! how eager is woman
to be bewitched!

THE NICHOLLS
OF NESBIT STREET

Why has David Bryant vanished, leaving his small daughter, Naomi, to be cared for by kindly Emma Nicholls? Who can be sheltering the missing man? How can Naomi, an only child heartbroken over her missing father, cope with life in a large, happy-go-lucky household? Angela Nicholls bitterly resents the intrusion into her home of both her grandmother and Naomi. None of them can foresee how Naomi's arrival is going to alter the course of their lives.

MARY LEDGWAY TEMPLE

THE NICHOLLS OF NESBIT STREET

Complete and Unabridged

ULVERSCROFT
Leicester

First published in Great Britain in 1992 by
Robert Hale Limited
London

First Large Print Edition
published August 1994
by arrangement with
Robert Hale Limited
London

British Library CIP Data

Temple, Mary Ledgway
The Nicholls of Nesbit Street.
—Large print ed.—
Ulverscroft large print series: romance
I. Title
823.914 [F]

ISBN 0–7089–3140–5

Published by
F. A. Thorpe (Publishing) Ltd.
Anstey, Leicestershire
Set by Words & Graphics Ltd.
Anstey, Leicestershire
Printed and bound in Great Britain by
T. J. Press (Padstow) Ltd., Padstow, Cornwall

This book is printed on acid-free paper

1

"I'LL be all right until Daddy comes, really Auntie. I won't touch the kettle or — "

"No lovie, I can't leave you on your own, but I'll tell you what, I'll take you home with me, and leave your daddy a note."

Kindly Emma Nicholls tried to hide her worry from the child. David Bryant was rarely more than a few minutes late, but the one night she had to be back — the night Mabel Nicholls was moving into 22 Nesbit Street, he was almost two hours overdue.

Quickly she packed a few things for Naomi. "Just in case you get tired," she told the worried little girl, and wrote a few lines for her employer.

With the ease of childhood Naomi soon forgot her anxiety in the thrill of a ride on a public bus, so different from the school mini-bus, or travelling in daddy's car.

Emma, easy going though she was, felt uneasy as they neared her home. The two younger boys would be all right, and Jeremy, her eldest, would be at nightschool, but Angela —

It was her eighteen-year-old daughter who gave her most cause for concern. She was working in a seedy cafe, her third job since leaving school. Emma had asked her to be home early to welcome her grandmother, but Angela rarely considered other people's feelings.

Eight-year-old Naomi held Emma's hand tight as they walked through the streets in the poorer part of the town. Emma's terrace house was a revelation to the young girl.

The boys, Laurie and Barry, were sitting at a littered table. Homework books had been discarded and were lying dangerously near some spilled lemonade. Naomi looked askance at the dog-eared pages and grubby finger marks. Daddy always made her be so careful. Bob Nicholls rose as they walked in.

"What's wrong, love?" Emma glanced at Naomi.

Eleven-year-old Barry had already taken

charge, though, and was demonstrating his skill at card tricks. Emma sat down.

"I don't know. David Bryant hasn't come home and I can't leave her on her own. I'm worried, Bob."

"You've rung his office?"

"'Siven's Office Equipment'? Yes, but no answer. What are we going to do?"

"We'll just have to keep an eye on her. I'll walk round to Hanver Square later and see if there are any lights on. Now you make yourself a nice pot of tea and I'll send Laurie to the chippie."

Bob knew his wife dreaded the arrival of her mother-in-law, but she was no longer fit to live alone, and there was no-one else.

Laurie, a year older than his brother, although not as tall, frowned when asked to go to the shop. Both boys were dark, with expressive brown eyes, but while Barry's twinkled with devilment, Laurie's were often serious. He took the proffered money and unhooked a large canvas bag.

Naomi smiled at him as he went out. Her ash blonde hair curled softly round her still baby face, with large blue eyes.

3

Already Naomi was finding how different life was here to the one she led at home.

Even Bob Nicholls had no idea just how much Emma dreaded sharing her home with the notably cantankerous Mabel, nor how deeply the loss of her 'front room' had hurt her.

True, the room was seldom used, but Emma had pinched and scraped to furnish it as she wanted. Emma loved to go and sit a few minutes on the settee and look at the arrangement of artificial flowers. To polish yet again the nest of tables and admire the rather garish flowers on the fitted carpet.

Now, everyone fed, and Naomi playing cards with the boys, Emma went into the empty room.

Mabel Nicholls wanted her own things round her, so Emma had pushed her own furniture into every available space in the large, old-fashioned bedrooms.

"Ridiculous," Mabel snorted. "You'll have all mine one day."

Emma hadn't said she wouldn't touch Mabel's belongings with a barge pole, but Mabel knew, and there had been a hint

4

of malicious triumph in her eyes as they met those of the younger woman.

Now Emma knew that her contented way of life of the last years had ended. Mabel she had known about, but Naomi — what if — ?

Emma loved Naomi. Not in the same passionate way she cared for her own children, but much as a small girl loves an expensive doll.

Emma had been employed in the nursing home where Catherine Bryant had gone to have her baby. Early complications meant a long stay and a strange friendship had grown up between the women. In the days before the birth Catherine had spoken of her fears that she would not live to care for her little one.

"Emma, if anything does happen, will you look after my baby? David and I are both only children, there's nobody else. Please?"

Emma had smoothed the fair hair from her brow and tried to soothe her, but in the end, to calm Catherine, she gave her promise.

So when the worst happened and David Bryant took his baby daughter home it was to Emma he turned for help.

She had never regretted making the change. David was a generous, considerate employer and over the years Emma had managed to save a small nest egg.

Emma had been overjoyed when her first child was a girl, but she soon realized Angela would never be the kind of daughter she had dreamed about.

The rows between them had been many, as Emma tried to dress her in dainty clothes, to curl her straight, lank hair. When Angela, tall, secretive, with none of her mother's gentle features, finally left school she was rarely seen in anything but faded jeans and sloppy tops. Her hair colour varied with her moods.

So far she had not brought any of her boy friends home, but just lately Emma had noticed a change in her. Her jeans were clean, and her make up not as heavy. But she had learned not to ask questions. Especially now, Angela seemed to resent her grandmother's arrival more than any of them.

Suddenly there was no more time for surmising. The van Bob had hired drew up at the door and soon the men were staggering in and out with Mabel Nicholls' possessions. Emma looked round the room, hating it as much as she had loved it before.

As the elderly lady, leaning heavily on two sticks, walked into her new home she gave not the slightest sign that she wanted to be here even less than her daughter-in-law wanted her to be. But she would start as she meant to go on.

"What right-minded person would put a bed there in that draught? Where are those boys?" She thumped her stick angrily.

As Bob and the boys began to move the furniture again, Emma guessed what Mabel's next request would be, and put the kettle on.

"Why does everyone sound cross?" Naomi asked.

"They're not really cross. It's just that, well, Uncle Bob's mother has come to live here and it's a bit strange for her."

"Can I go and see her?"

"Not just now. We'll let her settle in first."

Lame, short sighted Mabel might be,

but there was nothing wrong with her hearing.

"Who's the child you've got there?"

"David Bryant's little girl, Naomi. Her dad hadn't come home and I couldn't leave her on her own — "

She turned as the door was pushed open and Naomi walked slowly into the room. Not wanting her hurt by Mabel's sharp tongue, Emma put a protective arm round her. But she needn't have worried.

With the innocence of childhood Naomi walked up to the old lady. Mabel looked back, and slowly the old, leathery face softened and a smile touched her lips.

Mabel had always wanted a daughter, and her only son's choice of a wife had been a big disappointment; as was her only granddaughter. Now, looking at Naomi, Mabel knew she was looking at the little girl she had dreamed about.

She reached out and touched the soft curls.

"Naomi, that's a nice name for a pretty girl."

Naomi smiled back, and in those few

brief moments a friendship was formed between the two people who were to cause such disruption in Nesbit Street.

"I'll make you some cocoa," Emma said gently as she took Naomi back to the kitchen. But Naomi shook her head.

"I want to go home," she told Emma, and her voice trembled.

For once the kitchen was quiet. The boys were at a friend's, copying homework for the next day, Emma suspected. Bob had walked round to David Bryant's home, Bracken Heath, to see if there was any sign of his return. Emma drew the small girl onto her knee.

"We'll wait here till Uncle Bob comes, pet."

By nine-thirty when Bob came in Naomi's eyes were almost closing. Emma gathered her up to take her to bed, but Naomi struggled away. She was suddenly afraid — her father had always been with her.

"We'll tell him to come for you in the morning," Emma told her. Naomi, though, would not be comforted and it was Bob who finally carried the child upstairs. His eyes were gentle as he tucked her into their own double bed. In a few minutes she was fast asleep.

"Well?" asked Emma when he came back downstairs.

"No sign at all, love," Bob said. "I'll have to go and make some enquiries. We can't leave it any longer."

But Bob came back with nothing to report, and they stood looking down at the sleeping child.

"What will we do, if — ?"

"Look love, it won't come to that. The police are sure to find him. We'll manage somehow, it will only be for a few days."

"Now you get down on the settee and I'll push a chair up to the bottom of Laurie's bed. I thought you were mad putting settees and chairs up here, perhaps it wasn't so daft after all!"

But it was late before Emma settled. She washed Naomi's white blouse and pressed her pleated skirt. Naomi wasn't going to be shown up at school, not while Emma Nicholls was looking after her.

When Angela came in she stood eyeing the closed door of the room that was now her grandmother's. Had Emma only known it, Angela's disappointment about the room was almost as great as her own.

It was now two months since Colin Ankers had come into the cafe where she worked. Angela, hot and tired had been unaware of the smudged mascara as she stood waiting for his order. Colin had taken a napkin and wiped it away.

"Nice eyes like yours don't need all that make-up," he had told her with a gentle smile. The smart retort Angela would normally have made was suddenly stilled as she looked into his caring grey eyes, almost level with her own.

Colin had come in every day for a week before he asked her for a date. They went for a meal to a small, but rather nice restaurant, and as the meal progressed Angela had her first real glimpse of his sincerity and quiet sense of humour.

Only when they were leaving did he touch her untidy, dyed hair with a light, teasing finger.

"You could be so pretty, Angela," he told her gently.

Colin, employed by a large building firm, went on taking her out. Angela bought one or two silky tops to lessen the effect of her jeans, and found herself missing him the nights he was studying.

Now, when she was on the point of asking him home, of suggesting to her mother they could have coffee in the front room, her mother had again upset her plans. How could she ask him into the big, untidy kitchen?

Angela didn't realize how thrilled her mother would have been to concede to her request — to entertain one of Angela's friends in her lovely room. Instead Emma felt the breach widening between them.

Now Angela stared at the school uniform hanging from the old-fashioned pulley drier. As though her mother didn't spend enough time at that big house, Bracken Heath, without bringing her work home.

It was not until the next morning Angela realized her mother had not only brought the washing home, but the child as well.

"For heaven's sake! As though there aren't enough of us here already!" she reacted angrily.

Naomi was upset when she knew she had to go to school without seeing her daddy, and faced with various cereal packets demanded grapefruit and a boiled egg — "like Daddy gives me."

"Look, pet, the boys are having these — just try them?"

"No! I don't like them! I want to go home for my breakfast!" Her words ended on a high pitched sob, and a commanding voice called from the next room.

"Get me some tea and toast and bring the little girl in here."

Emma was anxious and afraid, and not knowing what else to do, carried a tray through, followed closely by a tearful Naomi.

"There now, you do look smart!" Mabel told her.

Naomi actually gave a little smile as she looked at the elderly lady, sitting up in bed with a warm shawl round her shoulders.

"Hello, what have I to call you?" she asked politely.

"Well, most people call me Gran, but you could call me Nan if you like."

"Nan! That's nice. I haven't got a Nan."

"I hear you don't want any breakfast. Neither do I," Mabel lowered her voice, conspiratorially, "but Emma's brought me all this toast and she'll be cross if I don't eat it. I'll cut it into small pieces and each time you eat one, I will."

Few people would have recognized crotchety Mabel Nicholls as she talked to the young girl. She hardly understood herself — she only knew that this child evoked hidden longings, hopes she had thought long buried, deep in her heart.

The toast was soon gone and Naomi stood up to leave.

"I've some nice biscuits in a tin. We'll have some when you come home."

"Oh, but I'll be going to my proper home after school. Daddy will be back by then."

"Well, that's more than likely."

Mabel's eyes suddenly looked bleak, and Naomi sensed the old lady's disappointment.

"I'll come and see you, though. I'll ask Daddy to bring me."

Naomi leaned over and pressed a kiss

on the dry old cheek before she ran from the room.

Mabel lifted a hand and wondered at the tears welling up in her eyes. She, who never cried.

2

CRANTON Junior School for Girls had two entrances, one where the parents collected their children and one where the school buses drew up to take those who lived farther away, home. Naomi soon spotted the bus she usually travelled on, and, as her friends and the staff were used to seeing her, no questions were asked.

Somehow, Naomi was sure she would find her father waiting for her, and the sight of the lifeless house as she walked up the drive to Bracken Heath made her hesitate and think of the cosy warmth of her Auntie Emma's kitchen. But she and her daddy shared a secret. The hiding place for a spare key.

So far Naomi had not had to use it, but she remembered her father's instructions, and there it was. Soon she had the heavy front door open, and with an insight beyond her years, locked and bolted it behind her. Then, alone and waiting,

16

she gave a small sigh of relief. Daddy would soon be home and he would want something to eat.

The fridge didn't yield much, and try as she would she could not get the tin of beans open. It would have to be egg and bacon. The bread was dry, but if she fried it.

Emma was late meeting Naomi from school, but there were still a few mothers there, so she waited. Soon she was the only one left. Vague memories of extra music lessons Naomi had spoken of, drifted through her mind. It was a while before she plucked up courage to ask a man carrying the rubbish out about Naomi.

"Sorry, don't have anything to do with the young 'uns. But you can take my word they'll have all left by now. Probably find her at home when you get there," he added reassuringly.

But Naomi doesn't know how to find her way to Nesbit Street, Emma thought, but she does to her own home — Emma hurried to the nearest bus stop. The school was out of town and by the time Emma scrambled onto the bus, she was breathing hard, her fears rising.

When she arrived at Bracken Heath, knocked on the door and called Naomi's name, all was silent. Bob still had her key and there was nothing she could do but turn and walk away.

She was relieved to find Bob at home when she finally reached Nesbit Street.

"Bob, it's Naomi! I went to meet her out and she wasn't there. She isn't at her own home either — Bob, what are we going to do?"

They looked at each other. For that moment, even Bob was not thinking straight as he remembered the small, tear-stained little figure he had carried to bed the night before.

It was Mabel who shook them back to life as she stood framed in the doorway, looking grim.

"I thought the idea of coming here was to be looked after. Do I get any tea or not?"

"It's Naomi, Mum," Bob told her. "She's gone missing."

"She was going back to her own home. She told me," Mabel said abruptly.

"She told you that?" Emma could

hardly believe her ears.

"For goodness sake don't just stand there repeating everything I say and looking gormless! Get round there. Break in if you have to."

There were not many cars in Nesbit Street but Bob's mate over the road had an old Ford and he willingly lent it when he heard why they wanted it. It was a long time since Mabel Nicholls had prayed. There seemed little enough to be thankful for in her life, but as she watched the car move away, her lips moved.

Meanwhile Naomi heaved a sigh of relief as she heard Emma walk away. Now she could get on with preparing her dad's meal. It took her a while to find the frying pan, the bacon looked a bit tatty when she had finished cutting the rind off, but it would taste all right.

Carefully she lit the gas under the pan. Not too low, daddy might come any time and she wanted it ready.

It was then she heard a car coming up the drive. Daddy! But even as hope filled her heart, it died. Daddy's car didn't make that noise. Tears rolled down her cheeks as she peeped unseen out of the window. She heard the bolts rattle as they tried to push the door open. Then suddenly a drift of smoke wafted towards her.

Naomi ran back to the kitchen where the flames were already darting up the wall behind the stove. She began to scream. "Naomi, open the door. Pull the bolts back."

Naomi heard Bob's voice and tried to answer, but the words wouldn't form. All she could do was to stand with her back to the door and scream. Short, staccato bursts of sound that she hardly knew she was making. Her legs were suddenly paralyzed.

Only the choking smoke was real and the ever increasing flames. She turned and wrestled with the door handle, but her numb fingers had no strength.

"Daddy! Daddy!" she cried. "Come quick! I'm going to burn — "

Slowly she sank to the floor. There were no more screams.

Outside Bob yelled to his wife to call the Fire Brigade before he dashed round to the back. For a second or two Emma was unable to move. Surely someone would come?

Here, though, in the wide, tree-lined avenue, where the houses stood isolated in their own grounds, separated by oleander or rose-covered fences, no-one else seemed aware of the smoke or the echo of the terrified screams.

Emma's hesitation was only momentary before she ran, faster then she would have thought possible, up the nearest drive.

When the neighbour realized the little girl they had seen around was trapped, she sprang into action, yelling for her husband and running back with Emma to Bracken Heath.

To Emma the call for help had taken ages. In reality Bob had hardly had time to break the glass panel in the back door and feel for the bolt, but he was halted when there was no key.

Looking wildly round him, Bob picked up a clothes prop and smashed it through the kitchen window, rotating it so that fragments of glass fell out, leaving a gaping hole.

"Let me, I'm smaller," a voice said as

Bob Nicholls hauled himself up, but Bob shook his head.

"My job," he said briefly. Then, the jagged shards of glass tearing his clothes, his hands, he struggled through and found himself standing in the kitchen sink.

Immediately he had to fight against the choking smoke. His groping hands found a towel. Blindly he turned on the tap, soaking the towel and for a few brief seconds his finger squirted water in all directions, before he flung the wet towel round his shoulders. He bent low under the smoke and saw a small, huddled figure near the door. Breathing as little as he could, but unable to avoid inhaling the thick, dense fumes, he dragged Naomi hurriedly, even roughly away from the door. As he opened it with one hand, he scooped the child up in the other and found himself in the spacious hall.

There was no way he could close the door to contain the fire. Already the hungry flames were following them, licking at the door frame.

Bob stared round. Where could he

go? The outer door was locked, and even now he was fighting the desire to lay down, to give up and just let unconsciousness take over, but he knew that would be fatal for both of them. Closed doors faced him, but at least the fire had not got through. So intent was he on saving not only his own life, but that of the child, he didn't even hear the arrival of the fire engines and the ambulance.

Summoning all his reserves of strength he stumbled through the nearest door. Even as his bleary eyes tried to locate the position of the window there was a shattering of glass. Hands reached out to take Naomi and other, gentle hands helped him through the opening.

Somehow, as they lifted him into the ambulance, he managed to smile at Emma, allaying her fears when she saw the blood and smelt the smoke as she leaned over him.

"I'm fine," he whispered. "Looks worse than it is. Naomi — ?"

"She'll be all right," Emma told him with more reassurance than she felt as she looked across at the still figure in the arms of a young policewoman.

Bob's burns proved to be only superficial but he was kept in hospital for a couple of nights. The smoke had left him rasping, speech was painful and the doctor insisted he stayed under supervision.

Emma hovered between her husband and the small girl who was becoming so much a part of her life, but neither of them were in danger and when the policewoman suggested she ran her home, Emma had to agree.

Emma soon learned that it was not only kind heartedness that had prompted the policewoman to make the offer. Once home in Nesbit Street the policewoman accepted a cup of tea and looked round thoughtfully. "Naomi? Is she any relation? I understand her father has gone missing?"

The girl was young, feeling her way and asked the questions hesitantly. Even so, Emma felt a sudden fear, uniforms always made her nervous, and for once she was glad when the forbidding figure of her mother-in-law appeared in the doorway.

"No!" Mabel had obviously been

listening. "She is no relation, but then neither is anyone else by what we can learn. But the child has a good home here with people who care about her."

"But," the young woman stared at Mabel. "There are rules, regulations. And Naomi did get into the house on her own, and start the fire. It could have been much more serious."

"I know that." Momentarily Mabel's voice softened and her eyes clouded, before she returned to the attack. "But if you people would get on with finding David Bryant, instead of fussing about his daughter, she would soon be back in her own home.

"Now Emma, am I going to get a cup of tea, or not?"

The policewoman soon left and Mabel turned to Emma.

"They'll be back, or they'll send the social workers," she said grimly, "so we'd better be prepared. Now then! Where did Naomi sleep last night?"

"In our bed. I had the settee and Bob managed on a chair."

"Mmm, we'll have to improve on that. There's a camp bed at my place. Quite comfortable — when the boys come home they can go round and collect it. It will fit in Angela's room."

"But Angela will — "

"Never mind what Angela will say. I'll deal with her — and as for washing facilities, Naomi can use my cloak room."

"But you said, you insisted — "

"I know what I said, and it still goes, except for the child. She won't be smelling the place out with after shave or that rubbishy scent stuff."

Emma was silent. When Mabel arranged to move in, she had paid for the space under the stairs to be converted into a cloak room. There was a shower and wash basin, but she had been adamant that it was for her use alone. Now she was willing to share with Naomi. Emma had the feeling that trouble was brewing.

"You haven't even asked about Bob yet," Emma chipped in, feeling the need to assert herself, to show this formidable figure who was mistress of the house.

"Of course I haven't. I phoned the hospital and got the proper picture. He is my son, surely you didn't expect me to wait until you decided to let me know. I'm only thankful Bob's firm insisted on having a telephone installed when he was made manager. I suppose I am allowed to use it?"

Mabel stormed her way back to her own room, the brief camaraderie between them, over. Emma turned her thoughts to food, there were still the boys to think about.

Suddenly Emma remembered her terror as she heard Naomi's screams. Emma was not gifted with much imagination but the policewoman's words rang in her ears. What if it had been worse? What if Bob and Naomi had not been able to escape?

As reaction to the events of the afternoon set in, hot, unaccustomed tears rolled down her cheeks. Sobs tore at her throat. She buried her face in her arms, resting them on the old scrubbed table, and cried as she had not done for years.

Conscious of Mabel in the next room, Emma tried to stifle the sounds of her distress, but had she had magic vision, she would have seen the old lady sitting with tears running down her own lined cheeks as the thoughts of what might have been crowded into her mind. But instead of being united in their grief, the two women were as far apart as ever.

That evening, Jeremy and Laurie made their way round to their grandmother's terrace house. The neighbourhood was now run down but a few of the old families, like Mabel, clung to the only homes they had known. The thought that the small house, her own place, although devoid of modern day trappings, was still her own, was warm and comforting.

The rent was minimal and she paid it ungrudgingly, even sitting sometimes with the heavy key warm in her hands as she let her mind drift back over the past.

When the boys asked her about putting the bed up, she told them to leave it. Like Emma, she knew how Angela would react. Mabel felt there had been enough trouble for one day. She didn't even notice Jeremy's thoughtful expression as he handed back the key.

★ ★ ★

Emma wasn't the only one the police wanted to interview. The following morning Bob looked at the two uniformed figures with a wry smile as he tried to force words from his dry, rasping throat.

"There's so little I can tell you. I did report David Bryant missing, but — "

"Yes, well, we're stepping up our inquiries in that direction. We're concerned about the child, though. But for your quick thinking she could have been — "

Bob shook his head. Superficial his burns and cuts might be, but he was still in considerable discomfort, and had to make himself concentrate. He knew how being taken away from them would upset Naomi. He had to fight.

"It won't happen again. Naomi will stay with us until her father is found."

The arrival of the doctor cut short any more questions, but Bob was left with an uneasy feeling that things could go wrong. He lay still as his dressings were changed, then let himself sink into a blissful sleep of oblivion.

When Emma walked up to her husband's bed that afternoon she was astonished to find Angela sitting on one side, and a pleasant looking boy on the other.

Emma kissed her husband and gave a wide smile that included both of the young people.

"Mum, this is Colin Ankers. He comes into the cafe and offered to bring me here to see dad."

Emma looked more closely at Colin, liking what she saw, but, knowing her daughter as she did, her reply was non committal.

"That was nice of you, Colin. And how are you now?" she asked, turning to Bob.

"Oh, improving. The doctor insists I stay until tomorrow though."

"By the look of you, I would agree with them. I've just been to see Naomi and she can go home with me today. The nurse is just going to get her dressed."

Angela delivered another surprise. "We'll go along and help."

Bob and Emma watched their only daughter walk out of the ward, Colin beside her.

"Oh, Bob!" Emma turned to her

husband. "He seems such a nice young man, do you think — "

"Steady on now. Don't go building castles. The lass is only eighteen, she won't be making up her mind just yet."

But as he looked at Emma's face he knew she was already making plans. He sighed as he covered her work roughened hand with his own. They lapsed into companionable silence. He had loved Emma since he was at school. A perfect wife she might not be, but she was all he had ever wanted, and after all, he thought drowsily, he himself was far from perfect.

When visiting time ended he was still asleep. Emma bent and kissed him. Tomorrow he would be home. Somehow the house in Nesbit Street was empty without him.

Colin ran Emma home but wouldn't go in. Both he and Angela had to get back to work but he did make time to draw up in a lay-by and take Angela in his arms.

As they drew apart, Angela looked up at him ruefully.

"I still wish Naomi hadn't come to our

house. If she hadn't dad wouldn't have been hurt, and — "

Colin laid a finger on her lips.

"Angie love, you can't blame a young kid. She didn't ask her father to go missing."

"She did start the fire though. Dad could have been killed."

"And so could she."

"They're putting a bed for her in my room."

"Well, it won't be for long. Her father's sure to turn up soon. Oh Angie, be glad you have a home to share. A place where you're loved, where you can love in return. Don't waste time being angry about things that don't really matter. There are so many other pleasant things to talk about. Such as this."

Again he drew her to him. They hadn't spoken words of love, it was still too new, but it was there between them, a vital spark as their lips met. It was with real reluctance that Colin drove away.

Angela remembered his words as she stood looking down on the little girl who was fast asleep on the camp bed in her room. She fought against the rising resentment at having to give up her privacy, at having to put up with the now cramped space in her room.

She remembered the look in Colin's eyes, and later, when memories of the fire returned to disturb Naomi's sleep, it was Angela who reached her before she could disturb the others. It was Angela who cuddled her, who felt suddenly warmed by the child's trust; who, for the first time, felt the satisfaction of easing someone else's pain.

★ ★ ★

Siven's Office Equipment was run by three partners, Hugh and Paula Firth, who had moved, at Hugh's insistence, from smaller premises as their business prospered; and David Bryant.

David had joined the partnership shortly after his wife's death, assuming, quite rightly, that the flexible hours would give him more time with his baby daughter.

The arrangement had worked well. David dealt with essentials in the office and then took work home with him.

Now Hugh and Paula stood at an office window watching the police car drive out of sight. Hugh was the first to turn away, thumping his desk angrily.

"What on earth does David think he's playing at? Causing the police to come snooping round?"

"I'd hardly say that looking for someone who has disappeared is snooping," Paula burst out.

"So what? He's left us in a very awkward situation."

Paula looked at her husband. Once she had thought him the answer to everything. He had worked hard in the beginning and she had willingly put in hours of overtime, disregarding the fact that Hugh never offered to pay her for the extra work.

When he first began to take notice of her as a woman, she had been too thrilled to see the thin line his lips compressed to when he was displeased, how only his opinions, his needs, counted.

Too late she realized it was not a loving wife he wanted, but someone to run his home efficiently, to be there when he needed to entertain his friends. The

34

fact that she was also a good secretary had been, for Hugh, an added bonus.

She realized how often lately Hugh had been away from the office. How David had quietly dealt with the work that Hugh had neglected.

"And what about David himself? Don't you realize anything could have happened?" Unable to say more she turned towards David's empty office, but Hugh hadn't finished.

"I suppose when you told the police all the books were in order, you had checked the fact?"

"No, Hugh, I hadn't. But I know David and the last thing you could suspect him of being is a thief."

Hugh watched her walk away and his eyes narrowed. So Paula wasn't as immune to outside influence as she tried to make out. She was obviously fonder of David than Hugh had realized, probably more than she realized herself.

He must be careful. Paula was his wife; she ran his home perfectly, asked no questions and was useful in the office. He intended to keep it that way.

In David Bryant's office, his secretary,

Marcia Craven, was staring miserably out of the window. As Paula walked in, she turned, her eyes full of hope, but Paula shook her head.

"Sorry, Marcia, but there is still no news. I thought we'd go through that last morning again. We may have missed something.

"Now David answered a call just after nine o'clock, but didn't say who it was?"

"Yes, but it was a woman's voice, and I'm sure she said something about a copier, but I can't be certain."

"And he left the office about nine-thirty?"

"Yes," Marcia hesitated. "I don't know whether it means anything, but he was sitting looking at the calendar, and he had a letter in his hands. He seemed miles away, as though he was thinking about something. He appeared to suddenly come to life and left the office about nine-thirty, but you know all that."

"And this was all you found on his desk." Paula looked again at the scrap of paper — Mrs E. Harrison. "You're sure you've rung all those in the directory?"

"Certain, and we haven't a Mrs

Harrison on our books." She turned away but not before Paula had glimpsed the misery in her wide awake grey eyes. Marcia was only young, in her first job, and Paula knew how young emotions could hurt.

Gently she put an arm round the girl's quivering shoulders.

"It will all work out dear, things do. Meanwhile, will you run me off a copy of the accounts, then you can go home."

Marcia flashed her a grateful smile as she walked over to the computer. In her own office, Paula sat, her mind going over the facts.

She kept remembering Hugh's words. She would take the accounts home. Hugh would be out and she could check them there without any interference.

3

THE next evening Jeremy Nicholls found the courage to ask his grandmother a favour. "Gran," he began awkwardly. "You know your empty house?"

"I should do, I've lived there long enough. What about it?"

"Oh, Gran! You know how much I want to pass my exams, but it is just about useless trying to study here. I wondered — could I use your house? I'd be ever so careful not to do any damage."

Mabel Nicholls looked at her eldest grandson. Of all the boys he reminded her most of her husband, and the love that few would have thought her capable of giving.

But to allow him into her home. She looked round, and suddenly thought about Emma. Had she felt a little like this when she had to give up her beloved sitting room for her mother-in-law? For the first time she felt a stirring of pity for the younger woman, but no sign of it showed on her face.

"And what else would you use it for?"

"Nothing Gran, honestly. I'd just leave my things there and go when I had time. I do want to get on, make something of myself."

Jeremy rarely talked about his hopes, and as he tried to tell his grandmother his cheeks flamed. But she seemed satisfied. "Right! Tomorrow you can get another key made. But if I hear of anyone else even going in, that's the finish. Understood?"

"Thanks, Gran! Thanks!"

"And why are you looking like a cat that's eaten the cream?" Angela asked her brother when they met a little later.

"It's Gran!" Jeremy realized too late he should have kept quiet, but now the damage was done. Angela grinned.

"Hear that, Colin?" She looked at her companion. "Somewhere to go in the evenings at last."

"No, Angela. Gran said only me, or the deal's off."

"Gran won't know a thing about it. Anyway I've as much right there as you have — "

Colin saw her temper rising and Jeremy looked at him helplessly, his new found elation checked. Colin motioned him to leave them, then took hold of Angela's arms, forcing her to look at him.

"No, Angie! We're not going to spoil things for him. It sounds as if your grandmother means what she says. Leave Jeremy alone."

Angela shrugged out of his hold.

"So you're like all the rest," she flashed at him. "You think you can tell me what to do. Well, you're wrong Colin Ankers! I'm my own boss and don't you forget it!"

Colin watched as she half ran, half walked away from him. Almost he called her back, but, although his heart ached to hold her, to speak gently, he walked slowly back to his digs. Tomorrow she would have cooled down, be ready to listen to him.

The next night Jeremy let himself into his grandmother's house and spread out his books and papers. Later he would need light and heat, but it was a slot meter, so he could pay for it.

But Jeremy had reckoned without the curiosity of the roughheads who now made use of the old, empty buildings.

"I tell you it is! Jeremy know-all from Nesbit Street. Remember him at school? Always swotting — well, we'll show him now."

Before Jeremy could do anything there was the sound of breaking glass. Too late he remembered he had not locked the door, he stood up as it burst open —

Whenever Jeremy tried to think back the next few minutes were nothing but a blur. He recognized the three youths who burst in; heard the sound of breaking china; felt a blow to his chest, then his arms went into action, but he knew he was no match for three of them.

Then, suddenly, the invaders were being thrown out. None too gently they hit the pavement outside.

"And don't come back — remember we know who to blame if there is more damage, and you won't get off so lightly next time."

Jeremy looked at Colin Ankers.

"I thought you told Angela to stay away," he said with a grin.

"I did! That's why I thought she might be here. Looks as though I came at the right time."

"Definitely! But how did you — I mean one minute they were all over me, then they were gone?"

"Judo — I found out very early that if you're brought up in a home you have to look after yourself. I hate violence and decided judo was the best way out. Didn't know I'd remember the moves so well, though," he added.

The two young men looked round the room.

"Not a lot we can't fix," Colin said thoughtfully. "We'll have to nail that window up for now, and I'm afraid this is beyond help."

He picked up a piece of broken china, and looked at Jeremy, busy sorting his scattered books.

"The table leg's broken, but repairable," Jeremy decided. "Anyway I don't suppose Gran will let me come here any more."

"Mmm, I suppose if you don't tell her

somebody else will. Anyway, it pays to be honest."

Jeremy managed a smile. "Knowing the old girl I wouldn't put it past her to take a taxi to check on me one of these days. Besides, if Angela — " He broke off, but Colin only shrugged.

"I don't think she'd split — but if your gran finds out you've deceived her, that will be the end."

"Let's clear up and go for a drink. I think we deserve one after this. Do you know where Angela is?" Colin was sweeping up glass.

"No, I didn't see her last night. She'll come round, Colin. I should just give her a day or two to cool off. It's just that, well she doesn't get on too well with Mum and — "

"And she hates being dictated to," Colin finished for him, knocking in the last nail with a resounding thump.

As they sat with a shandy in their hands, Jeremy found himself talking easily to Colin, and decided his sister would be a fool if she didn't take the olive branch Colin was so ready to hold out.

Naomi Bryant sat up in bed and

watched Angela as she changed and applied her make-up, more heavily than she had done of late.

"Are you going out with that nice boy who was at the hospital?"

Naomi was happy again, or as happy as she could be away from her beloved father. Uncle Bob was home again, they hadn't been cross with her about the fire, and Nan had spent the last hour playing ludo.

She was quite unprepared for Angela's curt answer.

"How about minding your own business?"

Even as the words spilled out, Angela was ashamed. The small intruder had somehow wormed her way into Angela's heart, but the child's innocent question reminded Angela that an empty evening stretched out in front of her. But if Colin was waiting for her to make the first move, well, he would wait a long time.

Angela wandered idly round, then, feet aching after being on them all day, turned into a small cafe.

It was not until the waitress put a large beaker of coffee in front of her, that Angela really became aware of her surroundings.

It was not the cafe she worked in, but for all the difference in the lay out it might have been. The sizzling coffee machine; the tired looking sandwiches; the hot shelf holding a few forlorn pasties.

Inevitably her eyes followed the waitress. Tired eyes; feet obviously aching for relief from the flat, shapeless shoes. Make up which couldn't hide the pallor evening brought after long hours in such a place. A replica of myself, Angela realized suddenly. That is how other people must see me.

Is that the only way I can make a living, she thought rebelliously? Is that all the future holds? From somewhere in her subconscious mind came the memory of the hospital ward where she had gone to help Naomi dress. The friendly atmosphere, the sense of doing something worthwhile.

She could remember a girl in a dark green dress, pushing the tea trolley, and pausing to put an arm round a small patient as she helped her to drink.

The next day Angela was on a split

shift, so she had an hour or two free in the afternoon. Almost of their own accord her feet took her in the direction of the hospital. It was visiting time so no one took any interest in her as she walked around. Until a nurse with an arm full of case notes asked if she needed help.

"Naomi — Naomi Bryant?" It was the only excuse Angela could think of.

"I'm sorry, dear, but Naomi was discharged a day or two ago."

"I wanted some help — to ask something. The almoner?" Angela dredged the name from vague memories of hospital romances, and the nurse smiled.

"If you go to the office near the entrance marked enquiries, I am sure there will be someone there."

Eleanor Grant looked at the girl standing nervously in front of her and smiled.

"Yes, what can I do for you?"

"I wondered," Angela hesitated, suddenly sure there could be no place for her here. But the kindly lady was still waiting. "I wondered, what qualifications do you need to work here? In the hospital?"

"Sit down, my dear. That all depends — what qualifications have you got?"

"None," Angela retorted, her old bravado coming through.

"And what are you doing now?" Eleanor kept her voice level. Years of dealing with people had given her patience and she sensed Angela's need.

"Working in a cafe. Not a very good one, either."

"Well, there are quite a few qualifications needed to nurse, but you are still young. You have time to study. Of course there are other jobs. Ward orderlies, the repair room. What had you in mind?"

Angela had expected to be dismissed out of hand. Eleanor's gentle voice loosened her tongue and she leaned forward, talking eagerly. Ideas she hadn't thought about until then.

"So you'd like to work on the children's ward, and eventually nurse children. Well, I see no reason why you shouldn't. Look, I'll give you these leaflets and if you're still interested come back in a week or two. But give it careful thought, Angela. It won't be easy, but worthwhile things never are."

Angela left the room in a daze. At first she neither saw nor heard the young man in a porter's uniform. He touched her arm, and she turned, first angry, then surprised.

"Ricky — Ricky Black! What on earth are you doing here?"

"I work here!" He grinned. "But what about you? What's all that lot for?" he asked, pointing to the leaflets.

Angela had never really cared for Ricky Black at school. But here, in a sea of unfamiliar faces the sight of someone she knew warmed her heart, and she answered more freely than she would have done normally.

"I'm thinking of working here. Well, at least I've got as far as asking for details. Look, perhaps you could fill me in a bit — "

"Sure! I'm off in half an hour. Wait for me in the canteen."

"I can't," she told him. "I have to get back to work, but you could meet me afterwards. Ten o'clock Brad's Cafe. Know it?"

Ricky nodded. Remembering all the times Angela had snubbed him, nothing could have pleased him more.

But Ricky wasn't the only one who turned up at Brad's Cafe that night. Colin had waited until nearly ten o'clock before going to meet Angela. He was determined to talk to her, end their quarrel.

Angela was out a few minutes early and he arrived just in time to see her walking away with Ricky. He saw Ricky put an arm round her shoulders. What he didn't know was that Angela was almost unaware of it, her mind filled with other things.

"Tell me, Ricky," she asked eagerly, looking up at him. "What do ward orderlies do?"

Colin Ankers turned away. How wrong can you be, he thought bitterly; but even as he told himself he didn't care, he knew that Angela Nicholls had left a place in his heart that would be empty for a very long time.

As his sister carried trays and dished out tired salads; as Colin waited for the time to go and meet her, to tell her what fools they had both been; Jeremy Nicholls walked into his grandmother's room and sat down, looking at her.

"Well?" she asked. "I would have thought you would be round at my place getting some work done after all the fuss you made."

"I've something I ought to tell you. It was my own fault," he went on hurriedly. "I left the door unlocked and these boys I was at school with broke in. I —"

"You mean you had a get together?"

"Oh, no! Nothing like that. They just came, well, to do damage."

"Were you hurt?" Jeremy shook his head.

"No, thanks to Colin Ankers." He went on to tell her how Colin had thrown out the intruders, and saw his grandmother's lips twitch, but there was no relenting in her voice.

"And what was the damage?"

"A table leg and a broken window, which we can repair. But I'm afraid we can't repair this — it was smashed to bits."

He held out the head of a roughly made pottery dog. For a split second, Jeremy could have sworn the old lady was going to cry, but she recovered almost instantly.

"No matter," she told her grandson. "I never did care for it much anyway. What's this then?" she asked as Jeremy held out the new, shiny key.

"You said if there was any bother — "

His voice tailed off and Mabel saw the disappointment in his eyes. Again Jeremy reminded her of her husband, all those years ago. She looked at the key and thought of the one in her bag. Dark with age and worn so smooth that it slipped almost too easily into the lock.

"Here!" She folded his fingers over the key, an unexpectedly warm gesture. "If I'd heard it from someone else — or if you'd asked them round, well! As it is, off you go, but mind you work! I want to see results."

She withdrew her hand and tried to keep the old sharpness in her voice, then winced as Jeremy threw his arms round her.

"Don't you worry, Gran. Just wait and see."

Once Jeremy had gone Mabel looked at the piece of pottery, and stroked the

51

rough head of the dog with a gentle thumb.

"Sorry, Rover," she whispered.

There had been little money to spare when she married, but they had managed a few days in a caravan at Blackpool. How thrilled she had been when her young husband won her the ornament.

"I'll keep it for ever," she had promised. Through the following years the dog had been her most treasured possession. When she moved to Nesbit Street, she had fingered it lovingly, but it had seemed so right in its old place on her mantelpiece, part of the house she felt should stay undisturbed. So she had left old Rover in peace.

Now — she reached for a tissue, wrapped the broken head in it and, rising with difficulty, walked over to the chest of drawers. She hid it under some of her clothes. It would never do for Emma to see it, she thought — to know I was daft enough to keep an old broken ornament. She closed the drawer and brushed her eyes with her hand. Time Emma was bringing her some tea.

★ ★ ★

The morning after the police had paid their visit to Siven's Office Equipment enquiring about David Bryant, Hugh Firth was down early for breakfast.

The knowledge that his wife, Paula, had more than a passing interest in David, had forced him to think. He looked round at his comfortable surroundings; at the breakfast table, his favourite croissants, his egg done just as he liked it.

Paula had turned into just the kind of wife he had anticipated. A good housekeeper, an elegant hostess and an ideal secretary. Although he suspected she knew of his various affairs, he had never for one moment thought of her being attracted elsewhere.

He was drinking his coffee when he opened the inside pages of his newspaper. Hanver Square? Surely that was where Bryant lived? He went on to read the short paragraph about the fire, and how Bob Nicholls had rescued the child.

He closed the page when Paula came into the room. The less his wife was involved in David's affairs, the better.

53

Later, as they walked out to the car he looked at the bulging brief case his wife was carrying.

"Homework?"

"You suggested I checked over David's figures. His section is showing a good profit."

When they reached the office Hugh told Paula to go ahead.

"I've a client to see," he said by way of explanation.

She looked after him as he drove away. Once she had checked his accounts as well, known what he was doing. How long since he started keeping them from her?

She went straight to David's office. Paula put the files she was carrying away, then picked up a photograph from the desk. It was of a child. A pretty child with a winning smile. Suddenly, for the first time Paula thought how David's disappearance would affect this little girl. Who would be caring for her? Then the door burst open.

"Marcia!" Paula looked at the young, tear stained face in dismay. Marcia handed her the paper, open at the account of the fire.

"That poor little girl. Imagine how David would have felt if — "

Paula knew this was no time to show her own feelings.

"Pull yourself together, Marcia. Obviously neither the child, nor this man — Bob Nicholls — was hurt. Now I suggest we forget all about David Bryant and get down to some work. There's — "

But Paula did not find it easy to keep her mind on her work.

If David saw the newspaper cutting and realized how near his little daughter had come to being seriously hurt, surely he would come back? So if the next two days didn't bring him, it must mean —

Paula pushed the frightening thought away and concentrated on the child. It seemed that the Nicholls, whoever they were, were lapse in their care of Naomi. Slowly an idea took shape. If she could care for Naomi, it would forge a link, if, no — when, David returned.

When Hugh Firth walked into his wife's office, Paula motioned him to sit down.

"I've been thinking about Naomi

Bryant. She was almost killed — in a fire."

"How did that happen?"

"You didn't know about it? It is in all the papers."

"Paula, you know I would have told you if I'd known."

Paula knew her husband was lying. She spoke slowly. "I think we should have Naomi to stay with us. After all, David is our partner — we should do what we can to help."

Hugh walked over to the window. He didn't want a child in the house, but if that was the price he had to pay to keep Paula. There were always boarding schools if Naomi became a permanent fixture.

"I think we should. But you can't expect her to just come to stay with strangers, though. How about asking her round for tea?"

Paula stared. "You mean you agree?"

"Paula, my dear." Hugh walked over to her. "You know I only want your happiness. If that means having Naomi, we'll have her."

4

EMMA NICHOLLS was feeling disturbed. The social workers had just left after asking questions, lots of them. They had insisted on seeing the bedrooms, the sanitary arrangements, and they had asked Naomi things. This time Mabel Nicholls was out at the community centre.

Emma sighed. She had never thought the day would come when she felt the need for her mother-in-law's support.

At least Naomi had said she was happy with them. "Next best to being with daddy and I shall go home when his holiday is over — "

But Emma was still not sure she would be left alone, and when the telephone rang she picked the receiver up nervously.

"Hello! Am I speaking to Emma Nicholls? Good! This is Paula Firth from Siven's Office. David Bryant's partner."

"Has he — is he — ?"

Paula ignored the interruption. "I'm

ringing about Naomi. I thought it might help if we have her to tea one day. Is she back at school yet?"

"No," Emma told her. "She's going back on Monday — but — "

"Good!" Paula said again. "Tell her I will meet her out of school. I'll be in a blue Escort, but I will go in good time and introduce myself to her teacher."

Had Emma but known it, Paula was almost as nervous as Emma herself. She had thought of little else but having Naomi —

"Oh," Paula added as she rang off. "I'll run her home to you about seven-thirty. Nice to have talked."

★ ★ ★

Naomi looked round the Firths' home. It was bigger than daddy's, but it was so quiet. Paula hovered anxiously. Naomi had been good, too good. Her table manners were perfect, but she hadn't chatted, responded as Paula had hoped.

Already the room looked different. Naomi's crayons were scattered on the table. The doll Paula had bought sat in a chair.

58

She was watching Naomi in the garden when Hugh walked in. She saw his reflection as he walked over to the table and gathered up the crayons, pushing them out of sight.

He picked up the doll, then aware of Paula watching him, laughed as he put it back.

"Sorry, not used to things about the place. Where is Naomi?"

"I'm here! Auntie Paula says you're Uncle Hugh."

"Yes! I've brought you some chocolate. Aren't you going to eat it?" he asked as she turned away.

"No. I'm going to save it and give Laurie and Barry some. They live with me at Auntie Emma's and they play with me."

Hugh frowned. Naomi stood, stiff and watchful. He felt he was not making any headway and he had to impress Paula.

"Please, is it time to go home now?" Naomi asked.

"You can't, your daddy is still away."

"I mean home to Auntie Emma's. It's nice there."

Hugh looked round the luxurious

room. Mentally he compared it to the sort of place Naomi was calling home. His annoyance rose.

He knelt and put his arms round the still little figure.

"Naomi, Paula and I have decided you would be better here — "

He heard the sharp intake of breath as Paula spoke.

"No, Hugh — not like that — " but he ignored her.

"We have this big house and we can buy you lots of toys. You could stay as long as you wanted — "

He broke off. Naomi was pummelling him with her small fists.

"No!" she screamed. "I don't like it here. I want Auntie Emma, I want — "

Hugh hadn't intended to hit her, but his quick temper got the better of him. The slap rang through the room and Naomi went quiet for a second or two, staring at him. Then she began to cry, deep, unchildlike sobs that tore at Paula's heart.

She put her arms round the trembling figure.

"Come on, love. I'll take you home."

As she stood up her eyes met those of her husband. She knew that when she heard the sound of his hand against Naomi's cheek the last vestige of feeling she had for him, disappeared. He had stifled her hopes of ever having Naomi.

As she reached the door she looked back. The doll she had bought with such care, so many high hopes, still sat in the chair, its painted smile immobile. They left it there.

"Darling, I'm so sorry it happened. Uncle Hugh didn't — " Paula's voice faltered. What excuse could she give? Naomi said nothing, just sat, her blue eyes dark with apprehension.

Emma, anxiously waiting, came out to meet them.

Opening her arms she held the small, tear stained figure close. Naomi, feeling the soft plumpness against her own slim body, the strength of the arms holding her, felt safe again.

"Uncle Hugh slapped me, but I hadn't been naughty, Auntie Emma, truly I hadn't."

It was not often Emma's gentle expression hardened, but as her eyes met those of Paula Firth they were as cold as flint.

"I think you'd better go," she said. Paula shook her head.

"I'm sorry about what happened, Mrs Nicholls, but I would like to talk to you. Please, I won't keep you long."

Emma heard the quiet sincerity in Paula's voice. Without speaking she turned and led the way into the kitchen, still cluttered by the dishes from the evening meal. Emma didn't ask her guest to sit down, she just turned to her, waiting for her to speak.

"I want to apologise. I was too abrupt on the telephone but I was worried. You see when I wanted to have Naomi — " Paula glanced at the child and stopped speaking.

Emma went across and switched on the kettle. Unearthing two clean beakers she filled one with orange juice and one with hot, strong tea. Putting them on a tray, along with some biscuits, she smiled at Naomi.

"Come on, love. You can have supper with Nan."

Mabel Nicholls had never believed in

pandering to the young. Her own son had had a cuff over the ear when he needed it, and although she knew Emma disapproved, her grandsons had felt her hand on more than one occasion.

Somehow though, Naomi was different. The child had walked into Mabel's heart as though there had been a place waiting, just for her. When Naomi told her about the slap, Mabel felt her temper rise.

"Well now, you get your supper. I just want a word with Emma. Then if you want to finish that game we started last night, get washed and ready for bed. We'll play for half an hour. School tomorrow."

Naomi picked up her orange juice obediently. With the true instinct of a child she knew that Mabel loved her. Already the memory of her time at Paula Firth's house was fading.

Meanwhile in the kitchen Emma poured more tea and motioned her visitor to sit down.

"You don't have to apologise. I shouldn't have let Naomi go, not after what she's been through. It was bound to unsettle her, but I was worried about the welfare people coming, and — "

"And I didn't give you a chance to refuse. I was worried, too. My husband doesn't care for children and I wanted Naomi to come before he could change his mind. I know now that her place is here, but — "

The conversation was interrupted when the door opened, and Mabel Nicholls, leaning heavily on her stick stood glowering in the doorway.

"What's this about someone hitting that child? Was it you?"

Paula was not easily intimidated, though.

"No," she answered quietly, "it was my husband."

"Well remember this is her home and there is only one person who can take her away, and that's her father. Now if anyone lays a finger on her again, they will have me to deal with. Just remember that!"

The two women looked at each other as she left. "That was my husband's mother, and by the sound of it, he's here now."

Bob gave his slow smile and held out a

hand when he saw his wife had a visitor.

"I suppose you're Mrs Firth. I hope Naomi behaved herself."

"She was very good."

Bob nodded.

"Aye, she's a grand little lass. We'll miss her right enough when she leaves here. You'll excuse me while I go and clean up? A pal and I run a small repair business in our spare time and I've been busy. Mend all sorts of things. A little lad brought a rabbit hutch round today. Insisted on paying us, all of three pence. It'll be a goldfish bowl next I suppose," he chuckled.

"He's a good man," Emma said as she checked the meat pie waiting in the oven. "Works all hours, but always has time for the kids."

"Actually I wanted to tell you that," Paula hesitated, "well, if you need anything, you can get in touch."

"We manage fine. But there is that posh school. Mine just went to the local comp. I don't know if there is anything to pay — "

"No, the solicitor will be seeing to that, and if Bob would get someone to repair the fire damage, he will see to that as well. I'll ring him up. But Emma, you should have some money. No, don't be offended. I know Naomi is getting all she wants, but you should at least have what David was paying you. I could ask the solicitor to contact you, David will be still getting his salary."

"But where is he?" The words burst from Emma Nicholls. "Haven't you any idea? He might be — "

"Emma, I'm as worried as you. We haven't a clue. A name did crop up but it led nowhere. I'm so afraid."

A stifled sound from Paula brought Emma's eyes round to her.

"Emma, I care about him. I haven't told anyone else, although I think Hugh suspects. Oh, there's been nothing between us. I didn't know how I felt myself until this happened. Now I feel so helpless."

Paula sipped the tea, warming her trembling hands round the thick beaker. Why had she, usually so reserved, talked to Emma Nicholls? The answer was all around her. Shabby, untidy, this kitchen spoke of home, of love, more than any of the rooms in the house she had to return to. She felt Emma take the beaker from her, felt the light touch of her hand and heard the understanding voice.

"Mrs Firth — Paula. If you ever want to come and see Naomi, or," Emma hesitated, as though suddenly aware of the difference between this cultured, well dressed woman and herself in her flowered overall, "or just to talk, even, you will be very welcome."

"Thank you! If we do hear anything about David, I'll let you know at once. Now I must go. I won't go in to Naomi. Say good night to her for me."

The two women smiled at each other both aware that a new friendship was forming. Then Paula drove away and Bob tucked Naomi into her small, makeshift bed. Almost before he was out of the room, the child was asleep.

Paula Firth drove home slowly and her husband was in the hall when his wife walked in. He tried to take her hand.

"Please, Paula," he began, but Paula stood away from him, her eyes deep and unfathomless.

"Paula, I didn't mean to frighten

Naomi. It was just that, well, I knew how much you wanted her, how much it meant to you. When she seemed to scorn what we had to offer —

"I didn't want to hurt you. You know I never want to do that. Paula, you are my wife. We've built a life together — "

His dark eyes pleaded for understanding, he ran a hand through his hair and in spite of herself Paula couldn't help remembering how necessary he had once been to her happiness.

When he came and took her in his arms, she didn't return the caress, neither did she rebuff him. Lately she had felt so empty, so alone. For a brief period she had thought Naomi may be able to fill the void, but Naomi didn't want her. And David? If he had cared even as a friend, surely he would not have left them in the dark about his whereabouts.

Her husband was all she had. When he kissed her she felt no semblance of her old feelings, but she forced a smile as they went into the drawing room together. It was not often Hugh spent an evening at home.

The next day Paula made herself get down to work. It was about ten o'clock when the secretary called her into David's office.

"A telephone call," Marcia whispered urgently. "From a Mrs Harrison. She wants to talk to David."

Paula grabbed the receiver. "Hello? Yes, this is Siven's Office Equipment. How can I help?"

"You can't, not now. I'd like to speak to a Mr Bryant."

"I'm sorry," Paula spoke slowly. "He isn't in the office just now. Can I take a message?"

"You can tell him he has lost a good cash sale. He was supposed to see me a week last Monday about a copier. Made an appointment but didn't turn up. I just want him to know that empty promises aren't much good for business."

"Please, don't ring off. This isn't about the copier. We're afraid something happened to Mr Bryant on his way to see you. We must talk, or if you prefer the police will call — "

69

As soon as Enid Harrison realized what had happened, she was only too pleased to answer any questions and drove straight round. She was unable to throw any light on the mystery though, only confirming what they already knew. Except that theirs was a new business, not yet listed in the directory.

But at least the identity of the woman David had talked to was cleared up, and they knew he never arrived. It was purely to make conversation that Paula asked about the make of the copier Mrs Harrison had finally bought.

"Oh, I'm very pleased with it. Of course Mr Bryant said he would see we got some instruction, and the other firm didn't. The instructions were good, though. It's a Syndron."

Paula stared. "It can't be! We're the only agents round here."

"Well, that's the make. Ordered it through a newspaper advertisement. A local supplier. Anyway I hope you find your missing man safe and sound. You have my address if the police do want to interview me."

Paula frowned as she sat back at her

desk. It was disappointing that Enid Harrison couldn't help. But at least she felt as though they had taken a small step forward.

As to the other matter, if the distributors were selling their Syndron products through another firm, it would have to be looked into. But beside her worry over David, that matter faded into insignificance.

Paula, still unsure of her feelings, was reluctant to face her husband, but she knew he should be told about the new development.

His office was empty. Paula went through the glass panelled door into the office where the two secretaries were working.

"Sorry, but Mr Firth did say he might not be back in today."

"If he does come in, ask him to pop along and see me. Meanwhile, have you that file on college supplies? It came down here after Mr Bryant — Mr Firth said he would deal with it."

"We did have it. I think Mr Firth might have taken it into his own office, but I'll glance through these."

Paula wandered back into Hugh's domain and opened a drawer or two. She found the missing file and as she called to Jane to tell her, Hugh walked in. He stopped, visibly annoyed to find his wife standing over the open drawer.

"Is it necessary to check on me every time I leave the office?"

Paula did not attempt to hide her feelings. "I was not checking. I wanted the college file. County Hall have been ringing and we can't afford to lose any orders, Hugh — or to get slack."

He had the grace to redden, but held out his hand for the folder. As Paula handed it to him a slip of paper fell out. Paula must have lifted it out of the drawer with the file. Hugh picked it up and pushed it into his pocket, then, without opening it, handed the file back. He walked over to the window and stood looking out as Paula told him briefly about Enid Harrison.

"So the worthy David had lost us a good sale. You know, we will have to look for a replacement. We can't go on short handed."

"Hugh! Don't be ridiculous. We manage

for much longer periods when one of us is on holiday."

"Sorry, love. Just testing," he murmured. But his eyes were dark with anger as he watched her leave. In spite of his efforts, Paula was still carrying a torch for David Bryant.

He waited until Paula left for home, then went into David's office, leaving with a brief case full of papers.

Rather to Paula's surprise, Hugh was in for dinner that evening, but after the meal, left her and went into his office. Paula was puzzled. Hugh did not often bring work home with him.

As she sat alone in front of the television set Paula felt incredibly lonely and suddenly she had a vision of the Nicholls' kitchen in Nesbit Street. It would be full of laughter, voices, love.

She went up early to prepare for bed. As she tidied the bedroom she picked up Hugh's jacket to put it away, and noticed the little strip of paper she had seen him pick up in the office, just poking out.

Acting on impulse, she pulled it out, but looking at it, the list meant nothing to Paula. The names of a few pieces of equipment which the firm dealt with. But, remembering how careful Hugh had been to keep it from her, she copied out the names before replacing it in his pocket and hanging it up.

The same evening Naomi visited the Firths, Jeremy Nicholls was sitting in his grandmother's house studying.

He frowned when there was a knock on the door. When he heard his sister Angela's voice outside, though, he drew back the bolt.

"Angela, I asked you not to — "

"I know, Jeremy," she interrupted, "but I didn't know who else to talk to. Please, give me a few minutes."

Jeremy looked at her. There was something about her voice, about her expression he hadn't noticed before. This didn't seem like his brash, almost selfish sister.

Jeremy sat back while Angela curled up on the settee.

"I'm thinking of changing my job. Going to work in a hospital, as an orderly." She watched for his reaction.

His enthusiasm was immediate. "I think that would be great."

"But I would really like to nurse. Children, I think. Jeremy, do you think I could study? Get some qualifications?"

"Yes, if you're prepared to stick at it. I've always thought you had a better brain than you would admit. Look, I'll make a cuppa and we'll talk about it."

So brother and sister talked, as they had not done for a long time, and Angela was looking decidedly happier as she stood up and watched Jeremy tidy his books away.

"Right!" Angela said decisively. "The next free time I have during the day I'll go to see Eleanor Grant again and get some information on children's nursing. Then I'll pick the one with the least qualifications and go for it!"

"Correction," Jeremy grinned. "You'll choose the one you fancy most and go all out for whatever it needs. And talk to mum and dad about it, for goodness sake!"

"I would have talked to Colin," Angela confessed, "but I haven't seen him. I swallowed my pride and rang him, but there was no answer."

Jeremy hesitated, then told her he had

seen Colin a few days earlier.

"He told me the firm had offered him a promotion, a job as a supervisor on a big project thirty miles from here. He had to go straight away. He wanted to tell you himself, but couldn't find you."

Angela's eyes lit up. Jeremy forgave himself for the slight fib. Colin had wanted to see Angela, but was not sure of his welcome, after seeing her with someone else. But Jeremy felt that now was not the time to tell Angela that, and he knew that Colin Ankers cared for his sister very much.

"Colin was looking for me? I thought it was all over."

Her brother grinned at her. "Well, it's not, is it? That's been your trouble Angela, too fiery for your own good. If you're going to make a go of this nursing you'll have to learn to curb your outbursts a bit more. You are serious about this?"

"I'm serious about it," she replied quietly. "I've been taking a good look at myself, and I didn't like what I saw. I was afraid Colin didn't either."

"Oh, Colin likes it all right. It's just that — "

"I'm my own worst enemy sometimes," she finished for him.

"Come on, let's go home now. I'm famished," Jeremy said, not at all worried about the studies Angela had disturbed.

That evening Angela hummed softly to herself as she prepared for bed. She felt so much better after talking things over with her brother. She suddenly felt closer to him, more a part of the family than she had done for a long time. And Colin would get in touch with her when he came back. By then she might have started her new job.

She tucked the covers round the sleeping Naomi. After all, if it hadn't been for her, Angela might never have thought about working in a hospital.

It was two days before Angela could visit Eleanor Grant. Angela took pains with her appearance, a grey-blue dress and a loose black jacket. She kept her makeup to a minimum, and brushed her hair till it shone.

When her mother came in after taking Naomi to school, Angela was conscious of her quizzical glances. She had never found it easy to talk to Emma, they were poles apart, but as they cleared the dishes, she found herself talking, explaining her plans, just as she had done to Jeremy.

"I'm not sure, though. It will mean a lot of work."

"Of course you can do it, lass." Emma had welcomed her daughter's confidences. "Oh, love, I've wanted something better for you all along. I've never meant to be hard on you, it was just that — " She hugged her daughter as though she was a small girl again.

"Your dad will be that pleased! He'll be back when you get in."

When Angela stood again at the desk in the hospital, it was not kindly Eleanor Grant who met her. A young efficient, business like woman, carefully made up, her pen tapping impatiently on the desk, looked up at her, eyebrows raised.

"I wanted to see Mrs Grant — "

"Sorry, Mrs Grant's on sick leave. Can I help?"

Angela stammered out her request.

"I think you misunderstood," the

woman told her. "I'm sure Mrs Grant wouldn't have actually offered you a job. We require some qualifications or experience, even for an orderly. However, if you leave your name and address, I'll mention it to Mrs Grant when she gets back."

Angela saw all her hopes, her plans dashed by the young woman holding out a pen. Quickly she scribbled her name and address and left as fast as she could. Nothing, she felt would induce her to go back.

Only now, when the chance had been denied her, did she realize how much she'd built on a new career.

But she refused to cry. From somewhere she dredged up a vestige of her old defiance. At the next shop window she took a lipstick from her bag and outlined her mouth in vivid scarlet; added more mascara, and because she had nowhere else to go, made her way home.

5

ANGELA, relieved to find the house in Nesbit Street empty, sank into the old, shabby chair that was her father's favourite. Angela, to all outward appearances so hard, so able to hurl back anything that life threw at her, buried her face in her hands and cried.

As she thought of her future; of weeks, months, perhaps years spent pushing heated pasties and beakers of coffee in front of people; as she remembered Colin, who had gone away without a word, her slim body shook with the violence of her weeping.

It was not until she felt a gentle hand on her shoulder, heard her father's voice, that she realized she was no longer alone.

Bob Nicholls knelt beside the chair, taking her hand in his and putting his other arm round her trembling shoulders.

"Angel," he whispered the old pet

name he had used when she was small. "Angel, love — don't."

He looked down at her. Her eyes were soft and luminous through the mist of tears. Her eye make-up streaked down her face and the lipstick, applied with such defiance as she walked away from the hospital, was smudged to an inane grin.

"Is it the hospital job? Your mother told me about it."

Angela told him how her hopes had been dashed by the young hospital adviser, who had taken Eleanor Grant's place.

Bob was quiet a while, watching the changing expressions on his daughter's face. Then, not wanting to shatter these rare moments of understanding, he chose his words carefully.

"So you're giving up? Don't you see, the young one — well she can't be used to dealing with people, making judgements. She's doing things by the book. Now the older one, the first lady, is more experienced. She'll be able to use her own judgement as far as authority allows.

81

"Angela, if this is your dream; if this is what you want, don't let the first wave of the tide wash it away. Hopes are so fragile, and time passes. If you want it enough — "

Angela looked at him. Saw the pensive look in his eyes, heard the inflection in his voice. This was a side of her father she hadn't seen before.

"Did you have a dream, Dad?"

"A long time ago, lass. My own little repair business. Oh, nothing fancy, I knew I would never break eggs with a big stick. Just a well equipped work shop where people could bring their repairs. Much as I do now in my spare time — "

"You'd have to charge a bit more. All the people round here know you're a soft touch. What happened?"

"Oh, I married, you children came along. Somehow I didn't realize I had given up.

"But you, love, well, you've only yourself to think about."

He gave her a last squeeze and stood up.

"Look at that clock! You go and make

yourself respectable for work and I'll sort out a coffee."

Angela was almost ready to leave when the telephone rang. Her father smiled as he handed her the receiver.

"Colin?" Angela repeated, hardly able to believe he was actually there.

"Angela! How are you?"

"I'm fine! Jeremy told me you had gone to work away."

"I'm sorry I didn't see you before I left. I miss you."

"I miss you. When will you be back?"

Angela knew her words sounded stilted, but she could not possibly tell him how his voice had stirred her — how much she wanted him with her. Not until she was sure of his feelings.

"I don't know. The job's taking longer than expected. Angela, your voice sounds funny. Have you been crying?"

"Crying, me?" She managed an attempt at a laugh. "No, just a bit of a cold. I'm just going to work."

"Then I'd better not keep you. I haven't much time, anyway. We're away from phones mostly, except those on the job, but I had to come into town to see about supplies. I'll be in touch. Remember me to the others, and Angela — I — "

The line was bad, the words blurred as the pips sounded. Had he really said he loved her, wondered Angela as she walked to work.

Once there, there was no time for dreaming, but as she filled urns, buttered slice after slice of plastic covered loaves, she thought how differently she would have greeted Colin if she had been able to tell him she had the prospects of a worth while job, of building a better future, just as he wanted for himself.

What had her father said? If you want it badly enough —

Angela went to rub down the formica tables yet again. By the time she had finished the cloth was cold, sticky with the driblets of sauce and spilled food. As she plunged it into a sink of soapy water a feeling of revulsion washed over her. Oh, yes! She wanted that new life, very, very much.

Angela decided she would get in touch with Eleanor Grant as soon as she came back, then she remembered Ricky Black.

He had been kind, helpful — she could write to him and ask him to ring her when Eleanor was back in the office.

That decided, the girl went back to the work she had come to detest with a new feeling of hope in her heart.

Naomi Bryant was in bed when Angela went up to her room to write the letter. She was reading a book and took a great interest in Angela's activities as she began to write.

"You writing to that nice man? The one who came to see me?"

"No, love, it's to — well, actually it's a business letter."

Naomi let the book she was holding fall on the coverlet. Her eyes clouded.

"Daddy used to write business letters. He used to bring them home from the office. He had a computer and he sometimes let me write things on it for school. He was going to buy me one of my own." Her voice trembled. "Angela, when is my daddy coming back?"

Angela crossed over and sat on the small camp bed. She took the child's hands wondering what to say. It was over two weeks now since her father had disappeared and despite all their efforts the police could find no trace of him.

"We don't know, love," she said gently, putting her arms round Naomi, now weeping quietly. "But he will come back, truly he will and until he does you will be all right here with us."

"Doesn't Daddy love me anymore? Does he know about the fire? Did that make him cross?"

"No, pet, he isn't cross, and he does love you, very, very much. We all do. I think your daddy will soon be home with his little girl. We'll be able to tell him how good you've been. Now snuggle down or you'll be too tired for school tomorrow."

Angela dimmed the light and drew the covers over the thin shoulders. For a few minutes she sat beside the bed. Almost she could imagine she was in the hospital ward she dreamed of, comforting a child far from home.

Naomi had brought to the surface a depth of feeling, a fluency of speech Angela had not thought herself capable of. If she had had any doubts about working with children they were all forgotten. She had her dream and one day it would be a reality.

She heard the front door bell ring and stood up, slipping the letter to Ricky in the pocket of her lightweight jacket, intending to pop out to the post box. Her father was just going to call her.

"Angela, a visitor for you."

"Colin!" She stared at him. "Oh Colin! Is it really you?"

They stood in the shabby hall on the thread bare carpet, hands clasped, their eyes saying things neither of them were aware of.

"Angie! I was so worried after the telephone call. You sounded so distant. I was sure you had been crying."

"But I thought you were miles away. How did you get here?"

"Cadged a lift," he grinned, the old infectious grin she had come to look for. "One of the blokes — his wife was ill and the boss said he could borrow a truck. I'm being picked up at eleven. I'll just say hello to your folks and then we'll go out."

They walked by the river. There was a seat sheltered by the lee of the bridge.

Their first kiss was long and sweet, wiping away misunderstandings.

"What went wrong, love?" Colin asked as they drew apart.

"It was my fault," Angela said in a low voice. "I resented you telling me what I should do."

"No, I was wrong. I came to meet you out the next night to tell you so, but I saw you walking away with another guy. He had his arm round you — I thought — "

"Another boy?" Angela was puzzled, then she remembered.

"Oh, that would be Ricky Black. I haven't seen him since I was at school until then. But I have a lot to tell you — "

So she told him about her decision to change jobs, how helpful Eleanor Grant had been, and where Ricky Black came into the picture.

Colin was all in favour.

"No wonder you were upset. But I hope you're not giving in."

"No, I shall see Eleanor Grant when she gets back." Almost she told him about the letter to Ricky that was in her pocket, but safe in his arms, and with so little time together, she didn't want to risk telling him something he might not want to hear.

Just now she wanted only the warmth of his love, the knowledge that they were together again.

It was late when they left their seat, but Colin needed a hot drink before the journey back in the shaky truck. They went to a late-night cafe near the pick-up point. Angela slipped off her jacket and when she went to the ladies' room Colin picked it up. An envelope fell out. There was no way he could avoid seeing the address.

"Mr R Black." But Angela had just told him — he hesitated. Love and trust are inseparable — where had he read that? He heard Angela coming back and pushed the envelope out of sight. He felt her hand slip into his for their last few minutes together.

Then the truck was there. He kissed her, not gently, but with a passion he had not shown before.

Angela's arms tightened. "Come home soon," she begged.

Colin hardly noticed the discomfort on the way back. If he wanted to give their love a chance he must trust her. But however hard he tried the memory of that name on the envelope would not go away.

* * *

In Peebles, many miles away from the Yorkshire town where Naomi wept for her missing father, Gail Newby walked round her newly opened art gallery. She could still hardly believe her good fortune.

Brought up by kindly, but far from wealthy foster parents, the art gallery had seemed like an impossible dream.

Even so, after her course at art college finished, she spent all her spare time from her job in a photographer's, frantically painting. The results were good, but she was reluctant to follow her friends' advice and try and sell them. If only she could find a room, somewhere to show them to their best advantage.

Gail knew the exact location she really wanted. A stretch of rooms above some shops in Peter's Road. There was no way Gail could raise a big enough mortgage.

So Gail had resigned herself to letting the dream slip away. Until the letters arrived. Questions about her past; requests for any details of her identity; her birth certificate.

After verifying that the address of the private agent was genuine, Gail took her hated birth certificate from the drawer.

"Mother — Catherine Newby — age — sixteen. Father — unknown — "

As she knelt with it in her hand her mind drifted to the problem of who could be making the enquiries. Her mother's people, suddenly struck with guilt? Her unknown father, belatedly aware that somewhere he had a daughter?

Her mother had let her go to strangers when she was only a few weeks old. Now she didn't want help from any of them.

Gail had got on with her life and was proud of her achievements. Almost she put the certificate away. Curiosity and a faint hope, which in spite of her down to earth approach to life, lingered deep in her unconscious mind, that somehow, a mistake had been made, that she had been loved and wanted, made her slip it into an envelope and walk to the post box before she could change her mind.

Then, a few weeks later, a letter from a solicitor, Sydney Buckle, and a substantial cheque.

'My client knows nothing can compensate for the love that should have been yours through childhood, but your benefactor is a good man. You need not hesitate to accept his help. There are no strings attached and he will never expect anything in return.'

Gail carried the cheque around for a long time. Then came the day when her feet took her to the rooms in Peter's Road. If she accepted the money, the gallery would be hers — she need not sacrifice her independence. One day she would be able to pay the money back — she could look on it as a loan.

Gail wrote to Sydney Buckle, thanking him and telling him how she had spent the money. Then, just before her twenty-third birthday came another cheque to tide her over until Gail's Gallery began to pay its way. Overcome by her good fortune Gail had written another letter.

'*I don't know why you are doing this. Whether or not you are the one that should have been with me during the past years. If so, nothing can make up for the hurt of being discarded; but I can tell you that I am happier now than I have ever been. I will make a success of things, I know I will. Whoever you are, I will pay you back. For now, all I can do is thank you from the bottom of my heart.*'

Gail had forwarded it to Sydney Buckle with a request to pass it on. Little did she know she had thrown a stone into a pool that was to affect many lives.

Now she was dressed for an evening out with Graham Stanley. Graham had been in his last year at college when Gail was in her first. She had thought him wonderful, but far out of reach in any way but her world of dreams.

When he walked into her art gallery a few days earlier, ostensibly surprised to find Gail the owner, he told her her paintings were good, that she had grown into a lovely woman and asked her out to dinner. He was the type of man who gave meaning to the words, tall, dark and handsome. Now she was actually going out with him.

The meal was wonderful. Suddenly, as she sat soothed by the wine, lost in the delight of the plush hotel, the envious glances aimed at her handsome escort, Gail became aware he was talking about the gallery, the end room. One she and the friends who helped her, had not got round to decorating.

"I have some money, Gail, I could help with expenses, and use that room to display my sculptures. It would bring more people in, so it would help you as well."

Gail stared at him. A partner, someone else with a say in how the gallery should be run. That was the last thing she wanted. Besides, much as she liked Graham, what she remembered of his works of art, she certainly didn't like.

An instant refusal hovered on her lips. Then he leaned forward, taking her hand, smiling into her eyes. In spite of herself she felt the power of his charm, felt herself tremble as she withdrew her hand.

"I don't know — I'll have to think about it."

"Fine, but don't think too long. I've already got a showing prepared. There was somewhere else, but I think working with you would be rather nice — "

His eyes made promises. Gail, confused by the turn the conversation had taken, stood up to leave.

When Graham helped her out of the car, he made no suggestion of coming in with her. He simply dropped the lightest of kisses on her brow, ran a caressing hand over her hair and drove away.

Gail walked into her flat in a daze. But she knew, however much Graham drew her to him emotionally, she didn't really want anyone else in the gallery.

The gallery was her brain-child. But he had mentioned putting money into it. Perhaps she ought to think about his offer?

She sat down, tiredness forgotten as she remembered how kind and gentle

David Bryant had been on her twenty-third birthday. He had told her how he learned of her existence when her mother, his wife, had been almost ready to give birth to her half-sister, Naomi.

He told her of her mother's heartbreak when, during her last year at school the man she cared about had gone to Canada leaving her to cope alone. How she had lived with the grief of having to part with her baby, until, before she could bring another child into the world, she had felt the desperate need to tell her husband about the past.

"I promised we would find you as soon as she was strong enough, but that day never came. Then I was busy rebuilding my life, caring for Naomi, and the years just slipped away.

"I felt it was too late to try and see you, so I traced you and thought the money would put things right.

"Today, as I was making an appointment to see a client, I noticed the date. Your birthday. The years rolled back and I was with Catherine. Your letter was on the desk in front of me — I forgot everything but the need that came through the words of your letter — I just ignored the client, got up and drove here — "

They had talked a long time. She had given him a painting he admired. A moorland scene backed by mist covered mountains, with a small cottage nestling in the lee of a bridge.

Promising to keep in touch, he had given her a telephone number. Surely he should be told about Graham's offer?

* * *

Paula Firth glanced thoughtfully at her husband. There was a smug, satisfied look about Hugh she couldn't account for. Now, as she rose to get the coffee he held out a restraining hand.

"Just a minute, my dear. About David Bryant's accounts. You did say you checked them?"

Paula stiffened. She knew Hugh had guessed how she felt about the missing man, and was on her guard.

"Yes, they were all in order."

"In the end — yes. But did you notice this withdrawal, or borrowing, if you

97

prefer?" He thrust the figures in front of her.

"No, I didn't notice," Paula stammered. "But he must have paid it back. There were no discrepancies in the final figures."

"Oh, yes! He paid that one back, but not this one, the last amount he borrowed a month or so ago. I suppose you missed that as well?"

"I didn't have access to those accounts. They hadn't gone through the computer. But he paid the first one back, so he would have paid this one back if he hadn't disappeared. He will be able to explain — I know he will."

There was desperation in her voice as she saw Hugh's smirk.

"Do you think the police will agree? It's not just chicken feed, and they are looking for a motive."

"Hugh! You wouldn't — please."

"Perhaps not — yet! After all we have a good life style here. It would be a shame to have reporters disturbing us, police snooping round. Now, my dear, how about that coffee? Perhaps a brandy? Then we can talk plans. I think it is time we put all this behind us and got on with our lives. Go back to a little more entertaining? A little togetherness?"

He pulled her to him, kissing her with such force that she felt her lips bruising. But no love, she thought as she closed her eyes. No love.

The next morning Paula sat at her desk, feeling as though her world had fallen around her. Any half formed plans she had made for freeing herself from her empty marriage to Hugh Firth had been shattered.

'Oh, David! If you had only confided in me. Shared whatever it was that was troubling you.'

But there was no reason why he should. There had never been anything between them but friendship, centred on their business relationship. Now —

The telephone shrilled in her ear.

"David Bryant, please? Could I speak to him?"

"I'm sorry." Paula hesitated. It was a young voice, hesitant, as though unsure how her call would be received. "Mr Bryant isn't in the office just now. Could I take a message?"

"No, it doesn't matter. It was just something we talked about. I'll ring again."

"No!" Paula's voice was suddenly urgent. "Don't ring off. When did you talk? It is important."

"On my birthday, July the second. Mr Bryant came to see me. But I've got a customer now, I must go. Just tell him I'll ring back."

"No — " Paula's voice was almost frantic. "Please — " The line was dead. Whoever it was David had talked to on the day of his disappearance had replaced the receiver.

6

PAULA FIRTH stood as though her senses were frozen. As though time was standing still. Then feelings began to return to her numbed body.

Who was this girl David had spent time with before he apparently vanished into thin air? She had sounded so young, so unsure of herself. Why, oh why, hadn't she managed to get more out of her before she rang off?

Paula knew she should report the call to the police, but her husband's revelations the night before about the missing money, checked her. Hugh had not made any promises about keeping the matter out of police hands. He had ensured her silence by veiled threats, knowing the last thing Paula would want would be to see their partner branded as a thief. So far the disappearance had been only in the local papers, but it needed very little extra to make it appear in the dailies.

Somehow she had to follow the unexpected lead. Perhaps if she contacted David's solicitors — the girl had a Scottish accent, that might be a clue —

Paula knew she was clutching at straws; that deep in her heart was the fear that the girl was someone important in David's life. Age was not always a barrier to love. David was still young enough to rebuild his life, and Naomi needed to be cared for.

William Jackson, who so far Paula had spoken to only on the telephone, was elderly; his office carpet worn; the filing cabinet large, old-fashioned.

As Paula was shown into his office he rose with old world courtesy and drew out a chair for her, his gentle voice reassuring.

But he could not help. He knew of no Scottish connection his client might have, and when Paula, reluctant, but knowing she had to confide in somebody told him about the missing money, he shook his head.

"He must have been working through somebody else. But there is one thing I can tell you, Mrs Firth — I would stake my life on David Bryant's integrity. Whatever is wrong there'll be an explanation when he returns."

The assurance of his words, and the conviction behind them, after the way Hugh had condemned the missing man out of hand, broke down Paula's defences and for a brief moment a blur of tears contorted her vision.

"But there must be something we can do?"

He nodded. "There might be papers in his desk at home. I think in the circumstances we are justified in looking. Do you have a key?"

"No, but Emma Nicholls has. She's the lady I rang you about. The one looking after Naomi. She goes round to Bracken Heath to keep it aired. But the police have looked through his papers."

"Mmm, but they were not sure what to look for. Neither am I for that matter, but I am better qualified to find something than they were. Come on, we'll go and look Emma Nicholls up now."

"But I can't take your time up like this."

"My dear lady, my time is my own.

I delegate now, just hang on to a few of my special clients. And I'll tell you something else," he added, "I think they'll all heave a sigh of relief when I walk out for good. It is only natural. They have modern ideas, modern ways. They can't wait to get their hands on this office, wants bringing up to date, they tell me — "

He chuckled, an infectious chuckle that brought a smile to Paula's face. She liked William Jackson.

Emma was a bit hesitant about handing over the key, but Mr Jackson soon convinced her it was in David's best interests. As they drove out to Bracken Heath, Paula couldn't rid herself of the feeling that Emma was worrying about something. Something she hadn't wanted to tell Paula in front of someone else.

William settled down at the desk and began to go through the neat sheaves of paper, thoroughly and methodically. Paula wandered through into the lounge. She had been in David's home before, but only briefly.

The lounge was tastefully furnished. Large, cretonne covered armchairs, a deep rose carpet, the palest of green walls and curtains. A restful combination which was repeated in the gracious dining room. Catherine Bryant had been a real home maker. How David must have mourned her.

Upstairs Paula looked into Naomi's room. The sight of the cosy room; the dolls still lying on the small bed; the desk holding boxes of crayons and a chewed rubber; the fairy mobile swinging slowly in the slight breeze, brought Naomi's plight home to Paula as nothing else had done.

She picked up a snapshot of David and his little daughter. Naomi was looking up at her father, her eyes, her lips, her whole face alight with laughter. Naomi still laughed, but only then did Paula realize how differently the child laughed. Not with her eyes, or her heart. Paula felt a sudden sense of shame that she had concentrated so much on her own feelings and not enough on the little girl's.

Because Naomi no longer cried, no longer demanded to go home, the grown ups had assumed her grief had lessened, but the child had just grown older during the last two or three weeks; realized she had to accept what was happening — and Paula knew it was thanks to the Nicholls of Nesbit Street that Naomi had survived as well as she had.

There was instant coffee on the work surface, so Paula carried a cup through to the elderly solicitor. He looked up as she put it on the desk. "Nothing," he told her. "Nothing at all."

Paula dropped William off at his office, then suddenly remembered how worried Emma had seemed to be. Impulsively she turned and drove in the direction of Nesbit Street. Naomi would be still at school.

Paula handed over the key.

"Thanks, but I did tell you it would have done any time. There's one hidden near the house, in case Mr Bryant needs it." Emma broke off, turning and making a great show of filling the kettle.

"Emma, what is it? You're worried about something. Can't you tell me? Is it Naomi?"

"Yes, there's a concert at the school on Friday. Naomi is playing the piano, and wants me to go. How can I go? Imagine, me!"

"Emma, of course you must go. Naomi needs someone there and you're as good as any of them. Better than most, I would guess."

But Emma shook her head. "I wouldn't know what to do or say. Naomi might be ashamed of me."

"Would it help if I came along?"

"Oh, Paula! Would you? And help me over what to wear?"

"Of course — now what have you got?"

Emma had a deep blue two piece she had bought for a cousin's wedding. Paula pronounced it ideal and left Emma feeling, and looking, much happier.

Naomi played beautifully at the concert. Afterwards the younger pupils were given lemonade and cake, while the older ones passed round light refreshments for the parents.

The headmistress, Miss Kaye, came to speak to them and looked thoughtful when they said they were with Naomi Bryant.

"Naomi has been rather subdued lately.

Oh, her work's fine, but she doesn't join in things like she used to. Has there been any more news of her father?"

Paula shook her head.

"I did wonder if there was a money problem?" Miss Kaye was obviously choosing her words carefully. "Naomi refused point blank to go on the school outing last week."

It was Emma who answered. Emma with her head held high, looking straight at the headmistress.

"There are no problems about money, Miss Kaye. Naomi is being well cared for and the reason she didn't go on the trip was because she never mentioned it to us. Her school fees will be taken care of."

Miss Kaye laid a hand on Emma's arm. "I know that, my dear. It is just that I don't like to see her as she is now. You will let me know when there is any news?"

Paula dropped them at Nesbit Street but refused to go in with them. Naomi had been very quiet on the way home. When asked about the school trip she told them she didn't say anything because she didn't want to go away in case her daddy came back.

"I have to be here, you see," she explained.

"Now then, how did the concert go?" Bob Nicholls asked.

Naomi ran straight into his arms and burst into tears.

"Daddy didn't come. He always comes and I played my best 'cause I thought he might be there, but he wasn't. One of the girls at school said my daddy was dead, but he isn't, is he, Uncle Bob? He isn't!"

"Hush love. No, your daddy will come back, I promise you. Now dry your eyes and get ready for bed. When he does come we'll be able to tell him how brave you've been."

"Come and have a game first," Barry asked her. Both he and Laurie had accepted Naomi as a sister, and were upset by her tears.

"Yes," added Laurie, "and you can choose what to play."

But Emma shook her head. "No, Naomi's getting ready for bed. She can take her supper into Nan's."

"I wish Nan had heard me play,"

Naomi said wistfully, her breath still catching as she dried her eyes.

Bob Nicholls looked thoughtful, then quietly left the house. He returned in the early hours of the morning with a bulging parcel which he put in his mother's room. He smiled as he closed the door. Mabel, who complained she never slept had not even moved.

The next morning Naomi found the parcel waiting for her when she went in for breakfast. She was thrilled to find a small, portable keyboard.

"Now I can play for Nan and practise for when daddy comes home," she laughed.

Bob, who had had the instrument in for repair, with instructions to sell it if he could, was well rewarded for his late night in the workshop.

Barry grinned. "I can dig out my mouth organ, Laurie can get a guitar and we can make a fortune as the Nesbit Street Trio."

So laughter again bubbled through the Nicholls' home, but for adults it was surface laughter. Their thoughts were with the missing man. What was it that was keeping him from his home and the daughter he loved so dearly?

★ ★ ★

As Emma and the rest of the family were trying to console Naomi, Angela Nicholls left Brad's Cafe to find Ricky Black waiting for her.

"Hi," he greeted her. "Fancy a bite of supper?"

"Ricky," Angela said wearily. "I've just finished eight hours of serving food. I just want to go home."

"You did write to me — for information," Ricky reminded her.

"You mean — Eleanor Grant? She's coming back?"

"Well, if you don't want to eat, at least let me tell you over a drink."

Angela sighed. It was obvious Ricky wasn't going to answer her question so she went with him to a quiet little pub on her way home. Actually she found herself enjoying the ice cold lime and lemon and sat back in her corner, relaxing her tired muscles.

Ricky looked at her. She had pulled

off the confining ribbon she always wore at work. Her hair, now its natural colour and well groomed, fell in a cloud round her shoulders. Her eyes, accentuated by dark shadows of tiredness were deepest blue. Yes, he must definitely see more of Angela Nicholls.

"Well?" prompted Angela, disturbed by his scrutiny.

"Eleanor Grant is coming back on Monday. But I would ring and make sure she can see you. She's bound to be busy after her spell away, and the young deputy will be keeping an eye open."

"Thanks, Ricky. It's good of you to bother."

Ricky leaned across. "Look, Angie, you're working too hard. How about a run on my motor bike on Sunday? We could go in the Dales — "

Angela was shaking her head. "Sorry Ricky, but I did tell you I have a boy friend. He's going to try and get through on Sunday."

"Only try? If you were my girl I'd make sure I was around."

"He's working away. The supermarket they went to work on is finished, but the firm has been offered more work. They must be pleased with the way he's handled things."

Ricky shrugged off his disappointment. If she did get that job at the hospital there would be plenty of opportunities to see her. After all, an absentee boy friend should not be a problem.

Angela was sure Eleanor Grant would help her, that working at the hospital was once again a possibility. But this time she would say nothing. Except to Colin. He had rung several times since his flying visit, and on Sunday they might have the whole day together.

She knew he would be happy for her if she could realize her dream, but as she drifted off to sleep, other dreams took over. Dreams of a life with Colin. Dear Colin.

It was late Saturday afternoon when the police car drew up outside 22 Nesbit Street. Naomi was out shopping with Emma and Bob answered the door.

"In here," his mother called authoritatively. Bob, knowing that whatever it was she would have to be told, led the two policemen into her room.

The old lady's face showed little emotion as the police told them how a hang glider pilot, making a forced landing in a valley about thirty miles from Peebles had found the wreck of a car. It had been identified as the one David Bryant was driving. The words hung motionless in the quiet room. It was Bob who broke the silence.

"And Mr Bryant?"

"Nothing! Not a sign — "

Only then did Mabel Nicholls let her feelings escape. She appeared to shrink in her chair. Burying her face in her hands, the words broke out as though torn from her heart.

"That poor child! That poor, poor child!"

★ ★ ★

Paula Firth too, was alone in the house when the call came. She replaced the receiver with a shaking hand. The car found, but no trace of David. It was to be winched up early the following morning, Sunday.

When Hugh came in she made small

conversation during the meal. She did not want his company the next day. Somehow she felt she would learn something — and if she did it was better she was alone.

Hugh was still asleep when Paula drove away very early on Sunday morning.

Gail, in Peebles, was having a disquieting week. She was wishing she had not rung off so abruptly when she telephoned David's office. But, not knowing how much he had told his colleagues about his private life, she had been so afraid of embarrassing him she had not even left her name.

To add to her problems, Graham Stanley had been asking for an answer to his suggestion that he rent part of the gallery.

Time and time again, Gail had wandered into the room and tried to visualize it as it would look if Graham took over. But she could only see it as she, Gail, had planned. The walls plain except for one or two flower paintings. Low tables holding small porcelain ornaments; delicately carved boxes, and in one corner a glass counter displaying artists' materials.

Gail was sure she could make it pay. That it would help to tide her over until her paintings became known — now Graham wanted the room. Had offered her rent — what would David have wanted her to do? If only he would contact her as he promised. She fought back the fear that he had walked out of her life, that he had decided he didn't want the complications of a step daughter. Or a sister for little Naomi.

However Gail couldn't help her feelings lifting a little as she dressed to go out with Graham again. The heat of the lovely July day was fading. A soft breeze had sprung up and Graham had promised her a run out into the country — a meal on a rose clustered balcony overlooking the scented flower gardens.

The hotel was all Graham had promised. The food light and beautifully cooked, and Graham as attentive as she could wish.

They went back to Gail's home for coffee, but when they went upstairs, Graham turned, not to the living quarters, but the room he coveted.

"Just listen, Gail," he pleaded, throwing

the evening paper he had bought down on a small table.

"Black walls — "

Gail gave a cry. "No, Graham! It's not that sort of gallery — "

"Well, grey then. That's it. Pale grey at the top shading darker near the floor. Some coloured mobiles, and my sculptures arranged in small groups, with chairs so people can sit."

"But I told you, I have plans — " Gail outlined her own ideas, but Graham only laughed and pulled her into the long hall. "You can do all that out here. It's big enough. Look, I'll bring a few things round in the morning for you to see. If you say no, I'll just take them away."

She felt his lips brushing her eyes, her cheeks, before he found her lips. Somehow, she felt as though, without meaning to, she had agreed with him. Smiling, he led her back to the sitting room.

"Now how about that coffee?"

After he had left Gail picked up the evening paper he had thrown down. She didn't buy one. She was saving all she could, and working as hard as she did, rarely found time to even watch the television news, preferring a good book when she did have time to spare.

Feeling the need to relax before going to bed, she scanned it lazily. But an inside headline banished her weariness.

"Hang glider pilot finds missing car. The car has been identified as that of David Bryant, the missing business man — "

7

THE morning was damp and a thick mist hid the movements in the gorge. At the top of the crag only a handful of people stood waiting to see the wreck of a car being hauled back over the edge.

As it rolled drunkenly onto the turf a young woman broke through the onlookers and ran over to the policeman standing near the wreck.

"Please!" She gasped. "Have you found him? You must tell me!"

"Calm down now, miss — and who might you be?" the policeman asked.

"Gail Newby, I'm — " her voice dropped and the woman standing nearby, with her hands thrust deep into the pockets of her coat, couldn't hear the rest of the words.

Paula Firth had heard enough to recognize Gail's voice. This was the young woman who had rung up. The one David had been to see on that fateful day.

The policeman had taken Gail over to another official, and they were deep in conversation. He took her to the edge of the drop, pointing down. Paula could hear their voices, but not the words.

Gail watched the police cars, followed by the tow truck with its ominous cargo, drive away, unaware of anything else until she felt a gentle hand on her arm.

"Gail," Paula spoke softly. "I'm Paula Firth, David's partner. You spoke to me on the telephone. We have to talk."

Gail Newby turned, looking at Paula, her eyes blank. Paula went on gently. "I was sorry you rang off, Gail. I — we're all so worried."

"Yes, it was rude of me. But you know my name? Who I am?"

Paula shook her head. "I recognized your voice and heard you give your name to the police. We have to talk.

"There was a farmhouse a couple of miles back with a refreshment sign. Will you let me take you there? I'm sure they would stretch a point and make us a drink, even if they're not open."

Gail glanced at the bright red scooter lying nearby.

"I'll bring you back here, but we're both damp and cold. We can't talk here."

Paula didn't mention the lost, desolate look in the girl's eyes. It was obvious that David Bryant meant a lot to the girl in front of her. But she was so young, younger even than Paula had feared. But she mattered to David. Paula had to care for her. David would want that.

The farmer's wife took one look at their mist-wet hair, their damp clothes and white faces, ushered them into a small room and put a match to the fire already laid in the old iron grate.

"There now," she said briskly, "we'll not stand on ceremony. I'm May Castle. A pot of tea I warrant, perhaps a bacon butty."

Gail held out her hand to the warmth, but shook her head. "Just a drink," she answered. May Castle tutted her disapproval.

Paula lifted the big, brown pot and filled the two blue earthenware beakers to the brim. Gail, colour already returning to her cheeks, took it gratefully. May Castle smiled as she put bacon butties on the small table between them.

"If you don't eat them my laddies will," she told them.

Paula took one, and after a slight hesitation Gail followed suit. Paula waited until the plate was empty and the beakers refilled before she spoke to the girl she hardly knew.

"Gail, will you tell me all you know? Please?"

"I'm not sure." Gail was calmer now and had had time to marshal her thoughts. "I don't know what he would want — "

"My dear, David is missing. His little girl is pining for him. The police are looking for him, and we're in a mess in the office. And Gail, if money is involved please be honest with me. I promise I would never do anything to harm him — "

Gail saw the pain in her eyes.

"No," she agreed. "I don't think you would."

So Gail began to talk. Hesitantly at first, then, as the relief of sharing her worries eased her tense nerves, she told Paula everything, speaking finally of her joy when her step father had visited her on her twenty-third birthday.

"It was so wonderful, hearing about my mother and little Naomi. He promised to keep in touch, and then, suddenly — nothing."

Paula was conscious of relief flooding through her. She had been so sure this girl meant something entirely different to David. Never for a single moment had she thought of a step daughter. Now things were beginning to fall into place.

If only there hadn't been that second loan still outstanding on the books, there would have been nothing to fear from the police questioning. It was as though Gail read her thoughts.

"Paula, the police said they were coming to see me. What should I tell them?"

Paula hesitated, but she knew she couldn't ask Gail to be less than honest. After all, there was no reason for them to be suspicious about where the money came from.

"Just tell them what you have told me. And Gail, I am sure David will be found. He has to be," she added simply.

"I think so. You see when he came to visit me he admired a painting. Nothing special, hills and a cottage near a bridge. I gave it to him and he laid it on the floor of the car behind the driver's seat. There was no sign of it and I am sure it hadn't been thrown out. I know the car was smashed up, but the maps and a book were still there. I think he managed to get out and took it with him."

Paula just nodded. She didn't say how forlorn a hope she thought it was. That the painting probably lay deep in the ravine.

Gail went on talking. "But if he wandered off — if someone is sheltering him, why don't they come forward? Now they have found the car it is in all the papers, and they must have seen it.

"And David himself, even if he changed his mind about being involved in my life, how could he leave Naomi?"

"Gail. Just wait a few days. See what the police come up with next. The car is the first step. And Gail, you aren't alone. I'll help all I can, I promise."

In spite of the trauma of seeing David's battered car, Gail Newby drove back to

Peebles in a much more settled frame of mind.

She was immediately confronted by an irate Graham Stanley, standing amid an assortment of sculptures, boxes and a whole lot of paraphernalia. Fortunately the hall was large enough to accommodate them all, but the door leading to the art gallery was securely locked.

"Gail! Where on earth have you been at this time of the morning? I did say I would come round, and you agreed."

Gail wasn't sure that she had, but now wasn't the time to tell him. For the next half hour she helped carry the stuff upstairs, the pal who was going to assist having long since drifted off.

As they worked, Gail wondered how much she should tell Graham? Perhaps when the police had been she would know a little more. Until then it might be wiser to say nothing.

The thought of the money David still owed worried her. Although Paula had played it down she guessed that if it wasn't paid back, the police could make a case against David. She hadn't spent all the money from his cheque. Could she pay some back herself? Later, she would ring Paula and suggest it.

Meanwhile Gail had to admit that Graham's plans for the empty room made sense. She didn't want to spend more than she had to.

It was only when they sat down that Graham noticed the signs of tension in the face of the girl he was beginning to think about more often than he cared to admit.

"I'm sorry," she told him, "but I can't tell you," she said in answer to his question. "Look, just leave it for now. It isn't my secret. I promise I'll tell you as soon as I can. But I've been thinking — if you want that room, well, to be honest the rent would help, and I think you can make a go of it.

"I'm not impressed with modern sculptures and I certainly don't look forward to piles of bricks or motor tyres draped round the place, but I promise not to interfere. You will have a free hand."

Graham threw back his head and roared with laughter. In spite of herself Gail felt her lips twitching, as he assured her there would be nothing like that. But when Graham suggested taking her out for a meal to seal the bargain, she shook her head.

"Sorry, but I'm too tired. I'm going to do what I have to in the gallery, then have something on a tray and an early night."

Rather to his surprise Graham found a great tenderness welling up inside him. He saw the dark shadows under her eyes, heard the weariness in her voice and his arms were gentle as he held her.

"All right, little one. You know where I am if you want me."

Hugh Firth was out playing golf when Paula returned. She knew that although the police would interview Gail themselves, she should tell them what she had learned. She felt it would help to talk it over first and thought of kindly William Jackson. Although it was Sunday, she took a chance and rang him at his home address.

His flat was as old-fashioned as his office, but it was warm and comfortable. Paula watched as he poured two whiskies.

"A little early in the day," he chuckled,

"but I only indulge at the week-end, and as long as the boys don't find out."

Paula seldom touched spirits but after topping it liberally with tonic water she found the drink warming her. Slowly she told William about the latest developments. He listened carefully.

"There's nothing I can do today," he told her. "Tomorrow I'll contact Sydney Buckle and see what he has to say. Don't worry, my dear. The mystery will sort itself out."

But Sydney Buckle could not help. He produced the letters David had sent him, telling him an agency had found his step-daughter and asking him to forward the enclosed cheque to her on his behalf, followed by a second one some months later. He had emphasized that he did not want his name drawn into it. But where David had got the money he had no idea.

William rang Paula. "I'm sorry, my dear, but I don't see that we have any alternative but to tell the police everything."

★ ★ ★

128

The house in Nesbit Street was empty, except for her grandmother when Angela let herself in. The school holidays had started and her mother had taken the two brothers and Naomi on a coach outing to the seaside for the day.

"My — you're looking pleased with yourself," Mabel remarked when Angela went in to see her. "Finished work already?"

"I have to go in later," Angela fibbed. She had no intention of telling her family about her interview with Eleanor Grant. When her brother Jeremy walked in, she stared.

"I knocked off early," he explained. "Is there any mail?"

"Sorry, only junk stuff. Was it something special?"

"If you can call exam results special. Oh, I can't stand it if I've failed, Angie."

"Of course you won't have failed. Not after all the work you've put in. Anyway, I'm glad you're here. You can wish me luck. I'm trying for the hospital job again this afternoon.

"Oh, and Colin says he should soon be back home working and he'll stand you a drink. We had a lovely day yesterday. He borrowed a car and we went to Dalby Forest. It was so beautiful." Her voice was dreamy, and Jeremy smiled.

"Good luck on both counts," he told her.

Eleanor Grant looked at Angela thoughtfully.

"You haven't done anything more since I saw you?"

"Yes, I came to ask about working here, but — there was someone else here. She said there was no chance."

Eleanor frowned. "Mmm! Well it takes time to become a good judge of character, and we all have to start somewhere.

"We do need an auxiliary worker for a night duty. If the management agree I suggest you begin there and attend these classes once the autumn term starts."

She handed Angela a small book. "They are run jointly by the hospitals in the district and will give you a good base to work from. We will see how you make out, then take it from there. I'm warning you, it won't be easy."

"I'll work hard, I promise. Thank

you, Mrs Grant. Do you think there's a chance?"

"A very good one, I would say. Leave it with me and I'll ring you after the meeting next week."

* * *

In a wooded area near the Cheviot Hills was a small gypsy encampment. The three married men in the group had fine motorised vans, but their grandmother, wizened Meg Parker still clung doggedly to the old horse-drawn bow-top van her husband, Ned, had so lovingly restored in the early days of their marriage.

The interior of the van was richly decorated. Although the gold paint, the rich scarlet and deep blues were fading, it didn't take much imagination to picture it in all its former glory.

The marriage had produced one fine son before Ned, breaking in a horse for a wealthy land owner had been thrown and fatally injured. The son in his turn had fathered Meg's three grandsons before he too, died from the after affects of a fall from a building he was working on. Now

Meg travelled with her three grandsons and their wives and families. A happy arrangement that suited them all.

On the long upholstered seat, that came into its own at night as a bed, sat a man. The bandage on his head was almost covered by a gypsy bandanna. He wore a rough brown jacket and old moleskin trousers. His arm was round a small girl aged about nine, and she sat looking first at the kindly face of the man, then at the brightly coloured pages of the book they were holding between them.

Little Rose Parker had treasured the book a long time, using her vivid imagination to weave stories about the pictures. Now this stranger was reading her the printed words, helping her to pick out one or two words herself. Her eyes shone as she looked up at him.

She could not guess at the troubled thoughts sifting through her great grandmother's head as, without appearing to, she watched and listened.

Old Meg was a true Romany. All she had ever wanted to learn were the old gypsy traditions. The secrets of the countryside; the healing power of herbs gathered from hedgerows and fields. Once her fingers had been nimble at basket making, and the shaping of flowers from the thin strips of bark.

Now she watched the man and the girl. What was the curious affinity that had sprung up between these two? It was not simply that young Rose had been the one to find the stranger lying unconscious in his shirt sleeves, wet from the damp mists, with the blood from a wound on his head congealed, hiding the severity of the gash. Together Rose and Meg had manoeuvered him into the van.

Meg was on the point of moving on when they found him. She and Rose were to follow the others. The sons were well respected as honest, hard workers and for years the small troupe had spent the summer months in the foothills of the Cheviots.

Sam, the old thoroughbred, was already harnessed, and every trace of the old camp site removed. Old Meg had to follow the road her grandsons had taken, but Rose was quite capable of guiding the docile horse while Meg tended the wounded man.

Now, he was able to move freely; was kind, courteous, but unable to give himself a name, and, apart from occasional lapses into puzzled silence, seemed content with his way of life.

Only Rose appeared to mean something special. Old Meg saw the way his eyes followed her, how eagerly he greeted her, how he hated to see her walking away.

Now the soft sound of their shared laughter filled the van. Meg, suddenly alert, spoke more sharply than she intended.

"Done all your tasks, Rose?"

"Not all, Grandma. I haven't collected the wood yet."

"Then you had better get on with it. Your ma will soon be back, she'll need to cook the meal."

Tilly and Grace, wives of her two eldest grandsons, worked alongside their husbands in the fields and on the farms. Scarlet, the youngest wife, was to Meg's delight, like herself, a true Romany.

While the other two searched for wider paths, Scarlet was content about the site. Still nursing her youngest child she watched over the other tiny ones and filled her time following the old crafts.

Then, when the others returned she would wander off with her basket full of flowers, small wicker containers and combs and trifles bought cheaply at the supermarkets to sell to the housewives at a small profit.

The gypsy children had obedience drilled into them at an early age, and Rose stood up at once. "I have to go now," she told him.

When the child had gone the man, whom Rose had called Mister since the day they found him, rose slowly to his feet, smiling gently at the old gypsy. Picking up a basket containing pots of paint and some brushes he lowered himself to the ground and walked away.

Meg watched him cross over to the extra motor van the boys had recently bought. Old and shabby, but still strong and able to withstand the weather. While Seth, Tilly's husband drove the family van, Tilly now drove the spare one. A woman driving a gypsy van! Meg shook her head as Mister stopped and carefully selected a brush.

Under Seth's supervision he had quickly grasped the careful method of applying the beautiful colours to the intricate scroll work. One side of the van was already nearing completion.

Mister painted with fierce concentration. Meg went into the interior of the van and picked up a picture. A simple water colour of a cottage by a bridge. The stranger had refused to release his hold of the painting while Meg and Rose almost dragged him from the wood where he lay. Then up the bank and over the rough ground to the van. The picture was wet and its frame broken. Ned, Scarlet's husband, had spent a long time cleaning it and repairing the frame.

Mister would sit staring at it for long periods. Did the little cottage have a deeper meaning? A meaning that was eluding his damaged brain? If the potions she was using continued to help, would he remember?

Already his wounds and bruises were almost healed. She didn't need her grandsons to tell her that one day soon he would have to return to his own kind. But what had he been running away from?

Slowly she walked over to a drawer and took out a piece of newspaper. She had found it wrapped round some scraps of wool a householder had given her. She stared down at the pictured face of the man so calmly painting one of her vans.

Meg had never searched for learning, had never thought it necessary to send her sons to school, but now she wished passionately that she could read the printed words below the picture. Did it say Mister had done something wrong? That if was found he would be sent to prison?

To be shut away from God's countryside, the bright joy of a summer day, and the sound of the birds' song was the worst fate Meg could think of. Mister had somehow crept into her heart.

Rather than see him shut away she would seek out another tribe. A tribe that could hide him away where he would be safe for years to come. But had she that right? Who was this man? Dare she ask for advice from someone, or should she act on her Romany instinct?

8

WHEN Paula Firth, tired and dispirited, walked into her office, Hugh was waiting for her. He looked pointedly at the clock.

"So you've decided to show at last?" he greeted her. "May I ask what you find so absorbing that the interests of the firm take second place?"

"I've been talking to the police — with William Jackson." She hesitated before going on and her husband eyed her sharply.

"They've found David's car," she said flatly. "Surely you knew?"

Silently Hugh cursed himself as he remembered the unopened newspapers at home. He hated Paula being in a position to tell him anything, but he kept his annoyance hidden.

"And David — have they found him?"

"No!"

Hugh looked away, but not before

Paula had glimpsed the satisfaction on his face.

Quietly, keeping her voice carefully controlled, determined not to let her emotions get the better of her, she went on to tell him, as she had told the police, about how she had met Gail Newby, and so been able to tell the police where David Bryant had spent the fateful day.

"Well, well! Who would have thought it?" Hugh scoffed. "Our faultless David with a step daughter tucked away. One he thinks enough about to get into debt over. To run the risk of a prosecution. Now, you must agree — I hardly think a step daughter would warrant that sort of devotion."

Paula's quiet control could take no more. She sprang to her feet, her knuckles white as she grasped the edge of the desk.

"You're talking nonsense, Hugh, and you know it. You've never liked David, even when you asked him to go into partnership with us. It was only to get his expertise and tide you over financially. Now you're trying to blacken his name — to — "

She blinked back tears of anger as Hugh turned to her.

"He's blackened it himself. I don't need to. And the police? What are they doing about it?"

"I don't see what they can do. They'll be interviewing Gail. I don't think she will be able to help, but there might be something."

The tremor in her voice was not lost on her husband.

"I would say he's arranged this very carefully. Hiding the car in the back of beyond. It should be obvious even to you he's decided to move on. That he doesn't give a damn about the business, his daughter, or anyone else. This so called step daughter is probably up to her neck in it.

"As for him — well, he'll be living under an assumed name and laughing his hat off. He's defrauded the company one way, so why not another? Well, I've had enough! I'm going to the police to tell them about the missing money — then they'll realize he has a motive for this disappearing act.

"We can't go on managing one short

like this. One way or another he isn't coming back — not that I'd have him after this! We're down on orders, but I've got my eye on someone — "

"You know you're just jumping to conclusions and that they're all wrong. Anyway, we can't involve anyone else, not at this stage."

"And why not? Just watch me! Can you stand there and deny that the business is suffering? For heaven's sake we're losing money, woman."

Paula was unaware of her nails digging into the soft flesh of her palms as she faced him.

"No, I won't deny it. But why?" She flung the words at him. "Why are we suffering? Why are we losing money? Because you have been letting David cope with most of your work as well as his own. You're hardly ever around. Practically part time — I wonder why?"

"And what exactly do you mean by that?"

Hugh was blustering. Paula looked at his heightened colour and plunged on. It was too late to turn back.

"I don't know. I only know that you

seem to have other interests — that you are leaving more and more to your secretary."

"Isn't that what secretaries are for? Never heard of the personal touch? Of visiting clients — looking for orders?"

"Orders? What orders? You said yourself there was precious little coming in."

Hugh turned swiftly and grasped the other side of the desk, standing facing her. She saw the anger in his face. Anger even she had not thought him capable of. She sank back in her chair and he towered over her.

"Come off it! You don't care about the business. You'd do anything you could to white-wash the virtuous David's name!" he snapped, jabbing his finger at her. "Don't think I don't know why. You're like a lovesick teenager.

"Go on — why don't you admit it? You're in love with him, aren't you? Well, aren't you?"

Paula felt the colour drain from her cheeks. For a moment she hesitated as the room swam round her. Then she stood up and faced her husband, her eyes meeting his.

"Hugh, we haven't been man and wife for a long time now. Oh, I was soon disillusioned as to why you married me, but I did care about you. I thought we could build a good life together. But it isn't a wife you want — it's someone to run your home, someone to be there to entertain your friends, be at your beck and call. And someone to help out here.

"All you ever do is take, take, take. You don't know how to give. So you want me to admit it? Yes, I am in love with David. I didn't know it until this happened, but now I'm sure. I love him, and I don't care who knows it. I don't care if he knows it, even though he isn't in love with me."

"Of course he isn't in love with you. Would he have acted like this if he even valued your opinion of him? No, Paula, I've told you before — you're my wife and it's going to stay that way."

The ringing of the telephone silenced him. For a few seconds neither of them moved, then Hugh snatched it up.

"Yes," he said curtly. "Hugh Firth speaking."

He listened carefully to what was said, then slowly replaced the receiver, and looked, almost with a hint of triumph, at Paula.

"The police. Just wanting to tell us that they've found David's jacket in the woods. Apparently it was rolled up as though he had been using it as a pillow. His wallet and papers are still intact."

His eyes were hard as he watched his wife sink back in her chair, her face, if possible, whiter than before.

"Another red herring," he said silkily. "I wonder what they will find in the woods next?"

He stormed out. Paula listened to his footsteps on the stairs, the slamming of his office door.

So it was all out in the open. Hugh's malice, and her feelings towards him. At least it made what she intended to do easier. Earlier, she had been reluctant to spy on her husband. Now that reluctance was gone. She was doubly sure her suspicions about him had been correct.

Just what did Hugh's absences from the office mean? She was convinced the list she had picked up in his office was connected. She unlocked a drawer and took out the copy she had made, studying it carefully. She remembered Enid Harrison saying she had bought a Syndron Copier, in spite of the fact they had the sole right of sales. She would start there.

First she crossed to the percolator and poured herself a cup of coffee, sitting until her nerves quieted a little.

Then, her fingers steady, she dialled Enid Harrison's number. "Hello, Mrs Firth! Nice to hear from you. You want to know where I bought my copier?"

"If you don't mind. We're having trouble getting one repaired and I thought they may be able to help."

"Well, it's only a small concern, I understand. I haven't been in touch with them since, but I'll give you their number."

Paula scribbled it down. They talked a while longer. Enid was following the case of the missing man closely and wanted to hear all Paula could tell her.

Paula ended the conversation as soon as she decently could, and sat looking at the number. She had heard Hugh leave the building a short while before.

Her hand was steady as she dialled the number.

"Hello! The Office Reliant Company. Can I help you?"

It was Hugh's voice. He hadn't wasted much time. Paula replaced the receiver with shaking fingers. So Hugh was running a separate business. Probably most of it legitimate, but syphoning a certain amount of stock, unattainable through legitimate means, from Siven's. Probably far more than would cover the money David Bryant had borrowed.

Paula was still sitting at her desk when Marcia Craven walked in. "I hope you haven't been needing me, Mrs Firth. Mr Firth asked me to help out downstairs."

She hesitated near the desk. "Are you all right?" she asked.

Paula didn't answer right away. Her eyes wandered to the connecting door. If Marcia had been in her usual office, she couldn't have helped hearing the heated conversation between Hugh and herself.

So Hugh had intended to have a row about David all along. Paula's news about the car and Gail Newby had been just more fodder for him to throw at her. That things had got out of hand, and they had both said a lot more than he had intended, she didn't doubt, but he had had no intention of letting anyone else overhear his slanging match — of spoiling his image in front of the staff.

Paula looked up and saw the silent sympathy in Marcia's eyes. Hugh was fooling nobody. If only he knew what the staff really thought about him.

Suddenly Paula was sick of the whole business. The deceit; the backbiting; the need to keep up appearances. She felt the longing to be somewhere clean, where things were really as they appeared to be.

A picture of Emma Nicholls' kindly, honest face swam in front of her. Emma, who put the welfare of her family before all else.

"Sorry, Marcia, but I have to go out. Yes, I know things are in a bit of a mess, but — " a ghost of a smile crept over her face. "I promise to be good and put in a full day tomorrow."

In answer, Marcia leaned over, and gave her a quick hug.

"It's all right. Don't worry. Things will work out."

Emma Nicholls greeted her warmly, but looked troubled.

"It's Naomi," she explained. "My lads are used to the streets and playing fields, they've known nothing else. But that little lass —

"I keep her in as much as I can. Mabel plays with her. Naomi has found a side to Mabel I didn't know existed, and she seems happy in the work shop with Bob, but I can't keep her in all the time."

"Emma, stop worrying. You do your best, that's all that matters. She might get a bit rough round the edges, but once things are back to normal, she'll be fine. The main thing is she's well looked after and cared about.

"That's all that will matter to David Bryant. You knew they found his car? Well now they've found his jacket — "

Paula went on to tell her about Gail, but said nothing about Hugh's threat to cause more trouble for David. She would deal with that, if and when the time came.

In Gail's Gallery in Peebles, Graham

Stanley was troubled as he worked in his new quarters. The police had been in with Gail for almost an hour. He looked round him, at the room he hoped would be the first step on the ladder to success.

Would this thing that was worrying Gail mean that the gallery would not be able to survive? Graham felt that should be his chief concern, but to his surprise, it wasn't. His thoughts were with Gail. She had looked so nervous, so apprehensive when the police arrived. What on earth could be wrong?

At last he heard the unwelcome visitors leave. Gail leaned against the door and the utter weariness on her face told its own story. Graham led her back into the sitting room and put her on the settee. Gently he lifted her feet and tucked a cushion behind her.

"Don't move, I'll be back."

As she sipped the hot, sweet tea he brought her, he smiled. "You looked as though you needed that! Now don't you think you'd better tell me all about it?"

Gail read the concern in his eyes. She had thought a lot about Graham.

He was so — so attractive, and, she had to admit, had always liked to flit from girl to girl before anything too serious evolved. Most of the girls she knew would give a lot to be dated by him.

But just lately, since they had found a shared interest in the gallery, she had felt the bond between them strengthening. Since he was now paying rent for a part of the gallery, she knew he would have to hear the whole story.

Slowly she began to talk. Graham Stanley listened without comment.

"You do realize that if I have to pay the money back it might mean closing the gallery? If it had had time to get known, to begin to pay its way, well — it would have been different."

For just a few brief moments Graham felt the injustice of it. He knew he was good, that if he could get a start he could do great things, and here was this golden opportunity in danger of being snatched away. He leaned over and took Gail's hands.

"Don't cross your bridges too soon. If the worst does happen — "

He was interrupted by the telephone bell. He handed the receiver to Gail and she listened quietly, saying little before laying it down.

"They've found dad's jacket. His papers and wallet were in the pockets. That means," she added slowly, "that whoever is sheltering him might not know who he is. Unless he is well enough to tell them."

Graham looked at her, his eyes grave.

"Gail, I think you have to face the fact that perhaps no one is sheltering him. He may have met with an accident or be laying a false trail."

She stared at him. Although she knew he was only voicing the things other people would be thinking, hearing her fears being put into words, made them loom much larger. She shook her head emphatically.

"The accident may be possible. But a false trail, no! He wouldn't do that."

"Gail, he had known about you for a long time before he finally got in touch. You've only met him once — "

"And that's one time more than you have, so don't judge!" She jumped off the

151

couch and stood staring at him angrily.

"He's a good man, and I've made my mind up. I'm going to look for him. You can see to the gallery, or close it whichever you like. After all, if it hadn't been for him, there wouldn't be any gallery."

"Gail, stop it — I didn't mean — "

"Oh, I know what you're worried about. Your precious sculptures! You're afraid the gallery will have to close. Well, if closing it would bring my dad back, I'd do that right now. And if he needs the money when I find him, he can have it.

"But I'm going to find him — "

"No, Gail! The police have everything to help them. You wouldn't know where to start."

"And do you think you have any say in what I do? Renting a room doesn't give you the right to control my life. I know exactly where to start. At Bracken Heath where he lives. I will meet my half sister, Naomi — "

"And bring more confusion into her life? How old did you say she was? Eight? How do you think she'll react to a strange sister suddenly appearing? Please, Gail! I'm not trying to tell you what to do, but I do think you would be making a mistake. I think you should give the police a few more days."

Suddenly it was all too much for the young girl. Tears she was helpless to check rolled down her cheeks. Graham took her in his arms, pulling her down onto the settee, sitting beside her, rocking her gently, stroking her hair.

Eventually her tears dried themselves, and Graham tilted her face to his. Their lips met in a long kiss, and when they drew apart, their eyes, full of wonder at this thing that had happened to them said it all.

"Everything will come right, darling. We'll make it that way," Graham promised. "And if the police don't come up with anything in a day or so, we'll both go and look for your father.

"As for the gallery, if it has to close we'll make a fresh start somewhere else, together. That's what matters now."

★ ★ ★

In the woods near the gypsy encampment old Meg Harper sat watching her great granddaughter, Rose, and the stranger they addressed as Mister.

He was sitting on the end of an old tree trunk, his arm round Rose as she proudly showed him the wild herbs she had gathered from the hedgerows. Herbs her great grandmother had taught her to know and understand. Now Rose was looking up at him, her eyes, as well as her lips, asking a question.

"You called me Naomi again, and I'm Rose. Do you have a little girl called Naomi?"

Old Meg held her breath as they waited for his answer, but it was slow in coming.

"I don't know, Rose. Sometimes I think she's there, then she's gone. Like a shadow, so many shadows," he whispered, his voice so low that Meg had to strain to hear.

"Does she live in a house? A proper house, with doors and windows?"

Again Mister hesitated, shading his eyes with his hand.

"Yes, I think so. There are flowers and

someone else — and a car. Yes, a car, but I don't know where to go — it's all dark."

He shuddered and buried his face in his hands.

Meg stood up and bent over him, urging him to his feet.

"Don't worry now, friend," she said softly. "It will all come back in time."

Mister walked a few yards, while Rose stopped back to gather up her herbs. Suddenly he turned to old Meg, grasping her gnarled, brown hands in his own.

"Meg, sometimes I get so afraid! What if I'm running away — if I've done something wrong and the police want me? If you get into trouble?"

It was the longest consecutive string of words to make sense that he had managed since Rose found him in the woods. And the fears he expressed were the one also filling Meg's mind.

"Steady, lad. Just give it a bit more time."

Back at the van Meg felt the rustle of the piece of newspaper in her pocket. She remembered how passionately she had wanted to read the printed words under the picture of this man sitting so quietly in her van. She had feared to show it to anyone else in case it meant that this man, whom she had come to respect, the man she had tended back to health, would be shut away.

Now she watched the changing expressions on his face. Occasionally he closed his eyes, and his lips moved, as though he was striving to recapture that part of his life which had eluded him.

Had the time come to show him the cutting? Would it jerk him back to remembering, or would the shock do still more damage? Wise though old Meg was, this was something of which she had little understanding and the thought of hurting this man, this gentle, kindly man, made her hesitate.

Meg stoked up the dying fire in the polished grate of her ornate caravan and foraged for food in the pan box beneath the floor boards. With skill learned over the years she added herbs, vegetables and meat to the contents of the large black pan. Soon, as she sat in the open doorway, savoury smells floated past her.

The next day Meg set off with a basket of wares of her own. She had been coming for many years and was well known, welcome in many homes. It was well into evening before she began to wend her way back to the camp.

It was as she was passing the ancient village church she met the old vicar, the Reverend John Soames. He stopped to talk, asking her about her family and how they had fared through the winter. It was as Meg looked into his wise, gentle face she came to a decision.

Slowly, for the paper was becoming very fragile, Meg drew the cutting from her pocket and handed it to the old man.

"Please?" she asked. "Will you tell me what it says?"

She watched as he looked at it. Saw the incredulity in his eyes.

"Meg!" John Soames looked at her, bewildered. "You know where he is?"

"He is at my camp. But if telling anyone means he will be in trouble, shut away — "

"No, he hasn't done anything wrong. Tell me a bit more."

John Soames listened, then sent Meg on her way, assuring her she had done the right thing, but warning her to say nothing, as yet, to David Bryant.

John was not a medical man, but he guessed a shock would be the worst thing for David in his condition. He went to the vicarage and dialled his friend, an elderly retired doctor.

Dusk was falling when the doctor's car drew up near the encampment. Meg led them across to her van. David lay sleeping, unaware of their presence.

"He sleeps a lot," Meg whispered.

"The best thing for him." He looked at John Soames. "I think we should let him sleep. Morning will be soon enough. But we must prepare his family."

As usual the gypsy camp was astir early. August was advancing gently. Early morning sunshine flooded through the open door of Meg's van. At a side table David Bryant sat eating the small breakfast, which was all he took. As he caught Meg's eye the slow smile she had come to look for lightened his haggard features.

Meg had tossed about all night

wondering if she had done the right thing. Somehow she felt she had betrayed a trust, for that was how she regarded this man who had come into her life so strangely.

But in her heart, she knew she could do no more for him. Bodily, he was healed, but how to untangle his clouded brain; how to restore his joy in living, without which no person's life can be complete, Meg didn't know.

He finished his breakfast and stood up. Crossing the floor, he took out his tray of paints, checking them carefully. Still not speaking, he made to leave the van, but as he passed, Meg leaned out and caught his hand, making him pause.

"David," she said slowly. It was the first time she had used his name, but there was no sign of acknowledgement in the eyes looking down into hers. Only puzzlement as though he wondered at the new mode of address.

She let his hand fall away. "Leave it to us," the vicar had said. There was nothing more she could do.

Meg watched as David walked over to the van the small band of gypsies were renovating. David began picking out the scroll work in bright, rich colours as though he had been doing it all his life.

It was work that didn't make his head ache with trying to think — a gentle occupation he could do at his own pace. Work that somehow quieted the distressing thoughts that sometimes chased themselves round and round his head.

Young Rose came running barefoot across the dew wet grass. Meg checked her, sending her back to her parents. Rose didn't argue, she was brought up to obey the older members of the tribe, but her almost black eyes clouded, and Meg spoke gently.

Rose was passionately devoted to the man who had read to her, taught her her first letters — Meg didn't want her there when 'they', as she thought of the vicar and the doctor, came for him.

It was about nine o'clock when the police car and ambulance drew up in the shelter of the trees, hardly visible to the camp dwellers.

A young doctor jumped down from the ambulance and joined the old vicar as he stepped out of the police car. When one of the policemen made to accompany them, though, the doctor stopped him.

"Please? We want to avoid a shock, if possible. Let us go alone."

The vicar detected the note of uncertainty in young Dr Francs' voice — if only the older doctor could have come. But David Bryant was police business, and as such a police doctor had to see him. There was little that John Soames could do except be there to support Meg.

John Soames gestured to Meg to stay where she was as Dr Francs walked up to the man calmly painting.

"Mr Bryant."

David smiled, shook his head and went on etching the gold paint in a delicate spiral.

"Please?" The doctor laid a restraining hand on David's bare arm. "You are David Bryant — you've been missing for several weeks. The police have been searching for you. I'm a doctor. We want you to come with us."

"No!" The word seemed torn from the depths of David's soul. It held a wealth of fear, of desperation. "I live here! This is my home — go away! Go away — all of you. Just leave me alone."

Old Meg, unable to stay away, tears rolling down her lined cheeks, ran up to him. She would have put her arms round him, but Dr Francs checked her.

"I'm sorry, Mr Bryant, but I must insist."

David dropped the brush, the paint tray and all the jars, and turned. He would have scurried away into the woods, but the doctor held his arm.

"Please," he said again. "We only want to help."

David shrugged him off. For a few moments he stood looking round wildly at the anxious faces, then a low moan escaped him as his damaged brain gave up the struggle. Before they could prevent it, he sank to the ground, blessedly oblivious as the ambulance men lifted him gently onto a stretcher and carried him away. Rose, thinking she had stayed away long enough to satisfy even her great grandmother was in time to see him taken out of the camp.

"I betrayed him," murmured Meg. "I shouldn't have told them."

Rose didn't understand. She only knew that her beloved Mister had gone. Meg and Rose comforted each other.

9

HUGH FIRTH was alone in the office when the police call to say David Bryant was in a Carlisle hospital came through.

Hugh managed to sound civil.

Yes, he would tell Mrs Firth, and anyone else. Yes, they would be in touch.

As he replaced the receiver though, his face was full of fury. He had been hoping David Bryant had gone out of their lives for good. But the police had said his condition was critical.

On impulse he went upstairs to Paula's office. He knew his wife was not there. She had received a call from William Jackson, just as they were ready to leave for work, asking if he could see her.

He stood looking round. He could hear the click of the computer as Marcia Craven worked in the other office. But Paula's office lacked the usual homely touches Paula loved. The flower vase on

164

the desk was empty, no plants adorned the window sill, and even the coffee percolator was not switched on.

For some reason, Hugh felt an unexpected wave of regret. As he walked over and switched on the percolator he was aware of the faint lingering of Paula's perfume. It was a long time since he had even thought of Paula other than as a necessary part of his life style, as opposed to part of his life. Suddenly, as he thought of a life without her, he felt unexpectedly bereft. Did she really mean to leave him?

With a start he pulled himself together. of course Paula wouldn't leave him, he was a necessary part of her life. She needed him more than he needed her. She would be lost on her own, in spite of her fine words.

He went back down the stairs. Paula was just crossing the hall. Silently he followed her up the stairs.

"Morning, Marcia! Have you checked the mail?"

So she didn't know David had been found. She would have told Marcia at once. Well, although common sense told him it was only postponing the inevitable, he had no intention of telling her just yet.

He could imagine how her eyes would light up, how she would rush to his bedside. No, David Bryant could wait.

"You look better this morning, Mrs Firth."

Marcia smiled as she placed the correspondence on Paula's desk.

Paula hesitated, then looked up at her.

"Yes, well. Look, I know nothing has been said officially, but I'm sure you and all the other staff have heard enough to know that there was a considerable amount of money missing. That David Bryant had borrowed it before — before he disappeared —

"Anyway his solicitor, a Mr Jackson, has found a cheque in David's mail for far more than the amount he owes. From a stamp dealer, apologizing for being so long, but saying he had been waiting for the right customer.

"Mr Jackson rang him and explained the situation and evidently David's late wife had inherited a very valuable stamp

166

collection. When David realized she had left a daughter, who needed financial help, he sold the stamps in two batches. Each time he jumped the gun, knowing the money would do more good if the recipient had it right away, and knowing he would be able to pay it back. His own money was tied up, a lot of it in this business."

"So it will be made all right?"

"Well, not yet — only David can do that. But as and when he comes back — "

Paula put a hand over the young secretary's.

"I think this is a good sign. I am sure he is going to be found, safe and well."

For the next hour Paula worked hard and the mound of letters was almost demolished when the telephone rang.

"Emma? Is something wrong?"

"Well, I thought you'd be coming round. Deciding what to do. Mr Bryant will need some clothes — "

"Emma! What on earth are you talking about?"

"But the police said you knew — that

Mr Bryant is in a Carlisle hospital — he's very ill."

"When did you learn this?"

"Just after ten o'clock. The police rang you first."

"Emma, I'll be round straight away. I didn't know."

Paula explained the situation briefly to Marcia.

"I will be taking Emma up to Carlisle. I wouldn't say anything to the others yet. I'll ring you from the hospital as soon as I know anything."

Before she left, Paula Firth went into her husband's office. As she expected he was not there, and she spoke to his secretary. "Did Mr Firth have a telephone call this morning? Around ten o'clock?"

Jane nodded.

"Who from?"

"He didn't say. I think it was something to do with Mr Bryant."

Paula knew she should be angry, but somehow, as she stepped into her car she felt only contempt, and in spite of herself that contempt was tinged with something akin to pity.

Emma Nicholls was waiting and led her straight into the kitchen.

"Have you told Naomi?"

"No! I talked it over with Mabel and Angela," she smiled at her daughter, busy preparing vegetables. "We decided, well, if anything did happen it would be better to say nothing for now. When we know — " she couldn't control her tears.

"Emma, love — we have to get moving. Where's Naomi now?"

"In with Mabel. But Bob will be home soon, and Angela's here."

Angela looked at her mother anxiously. "Would you like me to take her out today? I could take her on a bus to York. We could go on the river?"

Angela had seldom seen her mother weep, and was relieved when she managed a smile. "Thanks, love. Naomi would like that."

"Can I come?"

Laurie Nicholls had just walked in from his part time job, and Angela laughed.

"Laurie! It's not your sort of day out."

"I'd still like to come," he said stubbornly.

It didn't take long to pack a few things for David, and as Paula drove out through the gates of Bracken Heath, Emma spoke.

"Take me home, Paula. I'm not coming to Carlisle."

Paula screeched to a halt. "But you're all ready! Your overnight bag is on the back seat. Emma, you've a right to be there. David owes you so much — you've done more than anyone — "

"He doesn't owe me anything, but I've looked after Naomi all this time. She trusts me, and if she learns about her father I ought to be there. David will have you, and that other girl, Gail — "

"Angela starts her new job at the hospital tomorrow night, and Colin's away working still. Oh, I know it is so they can save up, and he wants to better himself, but Angie misses him. I should be there, she might need someone. She's never really needed me, but I still want to be there, in case.

"Come on, now, don't waste any more time. Just take me home."

"Very well." Paula drove through the busy streets. Surprisingly her thoughts were not with David, but the woman sitting beside her. As she leaned over to open the door, Paula spoke softly. "You're a good woman, Emma Nicholls."

Emma thought about the words as she walked into her shabby, comfortable home. To Emma, a good woman was someone who worked for charities, helped the sick, advised the poor. She had never thought of herself as good.

She went into the room she had so reluctantly handed over to her mother-in-law, and found the elderly lady sitting with tears pouring down her cheeks, a doll of Naomi's on her knee. Emma did something she thought she would never do. She knelt down and put her arms round Mabel Nicholls.

"We'll all miss her," she said softly.

"Oh, well!" Mabel pushed her away, but not unkindly. "She hasn't gone yet. What are you doing here? Thought you would be on your way to Carlisle by now?"

"I changed my mind, and came home.

I'll make us some coffee."

"Why not bring yours in here with me?"

The eyes of the two women met. They would never be close. Mabel would never quite rid herself of the feeling that her son could have done better for himself, that Emma had held him back. But at least she cared about people, and she had made Mabel welcome in her home.

As Paula left Yorkshire behind, her thoughts were mixed. So far, since learning that David had been found, there had been other things to consider. Now her thoughts could turn to the man laying unconscious in a hospital bed.

What if he thought she was trying to push in? Take advantage of his weakness? After all she was only a junior business partner. There must be others with more right to be with him.

But later, as she stood looking down at the thin, wasted form; at his closed eyes and the lines on his face, which even the veneer of sunburn he had acquired during his stay with Meg couldn't hide, she knew that no power on earth would make her leave him.

She bent over him, and in the privacy of the curtained cubicle, laid her head beside his; pressed her lips against his cheek; stroked the hair back from his brow.

"David," she whispered. "Please get well. Not for me, I know that is only a dream, but for yourself, your child. If love means anything, mine should be strong enough to draw you back. I just need to know you're there, somewhere — "

There was no one to hear the words, but surely someone would hear the prayer in her heart. She was still sitting when John Soames walked in and sat at the other side of the bed.

"I was with him when he came in," he said in answer to her silent enquiry.

In a low voice John told her about the gypsy camp.

"But surely they should have told the police at once? Once they found his car it was in all the papers and on the radio. They must have known."

"No, their way of life is different to ours. Old Meg didn't want to bring him suffering. She is the head of the tribe, and even if the others had heard anything, I doubt whether they would have told her.

"He had lost a lot of blood, and was very weak. I've come from the camp and the police had interviewed them all. They are quite satisfied that all was in order. Between you and me, I think old Meg probably did a better job of healing his body than anyone would have done. His mind though, well — "

"But wasn't there someone else? A daughter?"

"There's Naomi, but she's only eight. Then there's Gail, his step daughter in Peebles. I would have thought she'd be here — she will have been told."

★ ★ ★

But up in Peebles, Gail Newby was quite unaware that her step father had been found. Graham Stanley had arrived that morning, just as Gail was opening up.

"Gail! You look terrible."

Gail managed a smile. "Thanks! That's what every girl likes to hear."

"I didn't mean that, and you know it. But you can't go on like this. You're not sleeping, and you're not eating properly. Look, I have this friend just outside Lanark. He's switching from sculpting to painting and says I can have all his spare material if I pick it up today. Forget all this for a few hours. Come with me — we can picnic."

"Graham, you know I can't. There might be some word — "

He took her hands and drew her to him.

"When you do hear anything, what use will you be to your father if you're at the end of your tether? Come just for a few hours. Closing for one morning won't matter and we'll be back early afternoon."

Gail leaned against him, and smiled her consent.

"All right. I'll get a picnic ready," she decided.

"Oh, no you won't! This is my shout. You go and pretty yourself up and I'll slip to the delicatessen."

Graham avoided the main roads and chose quiet, winding lanes, some bathed in sunshine, some deep in shade from overhanging foliage. Everywhere the quiet beauty of the countryside they both loved surrounded them.

Gail lowered her window and breathed deeply of the soft air, letting the tension ease away. They didn't talk much, but her shared glanced with Graham said more than words. He was filled with a deep sense of contentment, as, his mission completed, he drove out to the foothills beyond his friend's home.

They carried the basket up the lower slopes and found a patch of smooth green turf dipping down to edge a clear burn, cascading gently over its rocky bed.

The food was delicious. Chicken legs, savoury patties and crisp rolls washed down by ice cold apple juice. To Graham's delight Gail ate hungrily, then stretched out on the grass, her head resting on Graham's lap as he leaned against a boulder.

Soon she was asleep, and though the time for their return had passed he didn't disturb her.

When, finally she did stir, he gathered her into his arms.

"Gail," he whispered. "Dearest, darling Gail."

Gail, still drowsy from sleep, returned kiss for kiss, until, catching sight of the time, she jumped to her feet.

"Graham! We should have been back hours ago."

The policeman was just walking away when they arrived home.

"We've been trying to get in touch all day," he told them.

"It's your fault I was out," Gail threw at Graham as the policeman left. "If I hadn't let you persuade me I would have been here."

"Gail, you needed that break. Now don't waste time. Pack a bag and I'll run you to Carlisle."

"You won't! I'll go on my scooter."

"You'll do no such thing," he insisted. "You're far too upset to drive safely. Besides, it will be much quicker if I take you."

Soon Gail was ready, but when Graham tried to hold her she pulled away, the closeness of the day was gone and they drove to the hospital in silence. Not the companionable silence of the previous journey, but the silence of two people far apart.

It was early evening when they drew up outside the still, grey building. The evening visitors had not yet arrived; and the afternoon ones were all gone.

As Graham opened the door, she looked at him, her eyes hard.

"If I'm too late. If anything has happened to dad, to the only relative I have, I will never forgive you Graham Stanley — never."

10

ALL was quiet as Gail Newby walked hesitantly through the open ward doors. The patients lay on their beds, in the half awake, half asleep state that comes early in a hospital ward. But Gail had eyes only for the occupant of the curtained cubicle.

Her stepfather lay motionless, his face in shadow, and for a moment fear welled up in Gail's heart that she was indeed, too late. But the hand she covered with her own, although limp, and apparently lifeless, was warm to her touch.

Only then did she look at the older woman, sitting so quietly beside the bed.

"Paula!" Her voice was low. "I would have been here earlier; I should have been earlier, but Graham insisted I went out — I'm so sorry — "

She choked back her tears. Paula managed to speak with a confidence she didn't really feel.

"It's all right, Gail. You're here now. You'll be with him when he comes round. He's going to be all right, love."

Gail looked back at David.

"Dad," she whispered. "Dad, it's me, Gail. Do you remember — "

Paula thought back to a few hours earlier, when she too, had spoken to the unconscious man. How she had said things she would never have uttered in front of a third person. Words she had desperately hoped would somehow reach David's mind, urge him back to awareness. Perhaps Gail would succeed where she had failed.

"Look, Gail, now you're here I'll just go and freshen up."

Paula walked slowly along the corridor and spotting a small side exit, she pushed it open and walked along a narrow hedged path.

To her delight the path led to a small, enclosed garden. The sky was not yet dark enough to be lit by stars, but the evening was far enough advanced to cast enough shadow to hide any deficiencies the garden may have. It was, for her, a place of peace, filled with the fragrance of roses and night wet grass.

Paula sat on a seat and breathed deeply, letting all the pent up emotions of the day fade away. Even so, her thoughts were still with David. How long would the lives of the people around him have trundled on in the same old pattern if they had not been jerked out of their way of life by his disappearance?

Gail Newby, who until that morning had not even been aware of her step-father's existence.

And the Nicholls of Nesbit Street?

Dear, kindly Emma, who had taken the forlorn Naomi into her already crowded home. Paula thought of the unlikely affection that had sprung up between the cantankerous Mabel Nicholls and the child. Would the hostility between Emma and Mabel ever have been bridged if Naomi had not walked into 22 Nesbit Street?

Through visiting Naomi in hospital, Emma's wayward daughter had had fresh thoughts about her future, and would soon begin her training as a nurse.

And she herself? Paula knew she had been pushing the thoughts of the future

181

to the back of her mind. Now, sitting quietly in the scented garden she faced the future with her mind clear.

Her life with her husband, Hugh, was over. But she knew he would not let her go without a struggle, so struggle she must.

Calmly Paula made her plans. Then, with a new peacefulness in her heart, she went back to the ward.

The nurses were just going in to attend to David.

"Why don't you two go for a meal?" asked the kindly sister.

Gail shook her head, her eyes on the bed. The ward sister laid a hand on her arm.

"He'll be all right, and you won't help him by not taking care. Go down the side street and you'll come to Sandra's cafe. The food's good and the prices there are reasonable.

"There's a bed here for visitors. You can take it in turns to rest when you're ready."

"Oh, Paula, I've been so stupid," Gail said miserably as they sat waiting for their order. "Graham was right when he insisted on me going out. Without that meal and the sleep, I'm sure I would have gone to pieces. I said some horrible things to him — "

Paula spoke reassuringly.

"Gail, we all say things we are sorry for at some time or other. Eat your omelette and then ring him. Don't just brood. Graham will understand.

"And," she added with a grin. "Seeing you've slept half the day, I'll take first turn in that bed sister was talking about."

* * *

David Bryant stirred uneasily, his brain reluctant to leave the world of oblivion that had cushioned him for the last few hours.

He was vaguely aware of gentle hands; but there had been other hands, just as gentle, but old, work roughened.

Briefly, in the half light he had thought Catherine was sitting beside him, but that couldn't have been.

Catherine had left him, but there had been a child — a dark child with coal black hair running through a wood,

183

taking his hand; but that was wrong again, his child, Catherine's child, had been different —

He tried to think coherently, but it made his head hurt, and he moaned, then, as always, came the prick of a needle and again, oblivion.

But the time came when he could open his eyes without the light searing them with pain. There was a girl sitting by the bed, a girl so like Catherine that he caught his breath in a spasm of pain as he remembered long forgotten days of desolation.

The girl leaned over, taking both his hands.

"Dad," she whispered. "It's me, Gail."

"Gail?"

"Your step daughter. Don't you remember? You came to see me, just before the car accident."

"Pictures," murmured David. "There was a picture."

"Yes, I gave you one — "

But David's mind was wandering again.

"There was someone else here, talking to me."

Paula had just walked in. She sat down.

"It was me, Paula Firth. Do you remember, from the office?"

He shook his head. "You were talking — "

"Nothing important," Paula assured him. Before she could say more, though, the doctor was there, urging caution, ushering them out.

"Let him remember himself. Prompt him by all means, but don't try to rush things. His body is healed, and soon his mind will mend itself. Now he has begun to remember it will all come back to him gradually. He has a long way to go yet."

By the evening David had recovered enough to sit up and take some food without help. Slowly he was piecing together the happenings of the last few weeks.

Naomi began to figure in his still hazy mind, and Paula reassured him about her welfare. She didn't tell him about the fire, or anything that might distress him, but she promised he would see Naomi within the next day or two.

That evening as they sat in Sandra's cafe, she told Gail she was going home. "David will be all right now, and I have neglected everything else. You have somewhere to sleep; you'll be all right?"

Gail nodded. "I shall miss you, but Graham says he will cope as long as I need to stay." She smiled. "I promised to ring again tonight. Let him know how things are."

So Paula stood beside David's bed and whispered good night. She longed to bend and press her lips to his white face, to will some of her own strength into him. Instead she reached out, touched his cheek and walked away.

It was late when Paula Firth drove through the impressive gates of the home she shared with her husband. First, she rang Emma to let her know how things were, then made herself a hot drink, and carried it up to a small, spare room and fell asleep almost at once.

The next day she went to Nesbit Street.

Bob Nicholls had just returned from his morning shift at the factory, and was mopping up the last remnants of his stew

186

with a thick chunk of bread.

He rose courteously and drew out a chair for her, smiling his own slow smile, while Emma added yet more water to the ever ready brown teapot.

They both listened carefully to the news about David Bryant, and Emma shed tears of relief when Paula assured her, her employer would be returning to Bracken Heath in the near future.

"Naomi? Does she know yet, about her father?"

Bob shook his head. "We thought it better not to say anything if we could avoid it. She's gone through a lot, it would have been cruel to raise her hopes.

"You say it will be all right for her to visit? We'll go on Sunday. I'll borrow a car and tell her then. You're welcome to join us. It would save you driving."

"No thanks. It's a kind thought, but I'll wait till he comes home now. I'll be at the office most of the time. Now tell me about the rest of your family. How's Jeremy?"

"Very well, thank you!" A laughing voice from the hall shouted back. "I've got a place at a college. Unfortunately it's down south, rather further away than I planned, but it's a sandwich course with a building firm, so I shall be able to pay my way and it's exactly what I wanted."

Paula smiled at the young man. It was nice to hear his enthusiasm spilling over after the harrowing hours at the hospital.

"And Angela?"

"She starts tonight! She's upstairs having a rest, but I think she's too nervous to sleep. I'm sure she'll be fine once she gets the first night over." Emma, anxious for her daughter, was assuring herself as much as everyone.

"You know I can't believe that Naomi will be leaving us before long. We'll all miss her, but it will be really hard for Mabel."

None of them heard the door open as Laurie Nicholls walked in in time to hear his mother's words. He was nearly thirteen and could not understand his feelings as he stood there. Naomi was leaving?

He turned and ran up the stairs to the

room he shared with Jeremy and Barry. He sat on the bed. A young boy who had grown up in a crowded, untidy home. In spite of that it was a home full of love.

In an area where he had to fend for himself, where many of his friends were rough, seeking only an easy way of life, he now knew he wanted something better than that.

He was still sitting when Jeremy came up. The older boy perched on the bed beside him.

"You're looking very solemn, Laurie. Anything you want to talk about?"

"Jerry, you're going to college. Do you think I could, or perhaps even to university?"

Jeremy stared. Neither Laurie or Barry had shown much inclination for study, but he soon saw the boy was in earnest.

"You can do anything you set your heart on if you work hard enough. Start now and get stuck in. Oh, some of the other boys will scoff a bit, Barry as well, but ignore them. You will find lots of others who will want to help."

"You won't be here."

"No, but the firm has a branch not

far away so I'll try and get sent there for some of the time. And we can write and telephone. Any time you want to talk, I'll listen."

"Do you think if I really work I'll ever be able to afford a house like Mr Bryant's Bracken Heath?"

Slowly Jeremy began to understand. But he didn't scoff, didn't tease. Instead he put an arm round his younger brother.

"If that is what you want when the time comes, yes. So it's a bargain. You work hard and I'll be on hand to help. Let's shake on it."

Solemnly they shook hands, sealing a new understanding between them, before Laurie scampered downstairs in search of food.

★ ★ ★

Angela Nicholls looked at herself in the mirror. The dark green dress of a hospital auxiliary, belted round her slim waist, was a sharp contrast to the mini skirts and jeans she was so used to.

The slight touch of make up she had allowed herself couldn't hide the anxiety in her eyes, the nervous flush on her cheeks. Tonight was so important. There were so many people who would feel let down if she made a mess of things, so many people who had helped her.

Her goodbye to Emma was brief, and she acknowledged her good wishes with only a curt nod, but Emma didn't mind. She was beginning to understand her daughter.

Angela had just left the house when she saw Colin Ankers walking towards her. With a little cry of delight, she ran to meet him.

"Colin! I thought you were miles away."

He hugged her. "I was, but got some time off. I kept thinking about you and I knew I had to be here, to wish you well."

Their kiss was long and urgent, and Angela held his arms as they began to walk.

"Everything will be all right, now," she told him, smiling. But they had hardly turned the corner when Ricky Black greeted them.

"Thought you might be in need of

a little moral support, but I see I was pipped to the post."

Angela felt Colin stiffen as he released his arm.

"Sorry if I've spoiled something — " he began, but Ricky interrupted. He knew when to accept defeat.

"Oh, come off your high horse. Angela didn't know I was coming, but you know me, always worth a try. Mind, I suppose I already knew I was flogging a dead horse. There was only one bloke who mattered to Angie. No hard feelings?"

He held out a hand, and after only a brief hesitation, Colin took it.

"And the offer of free advice if you want to know anything still stands," Ricky said as he turned to leave. "I may offer her a cup of soothing tea in the staff room — ?" he asked with a wicked grin, looking at Colin.

Colin burst out laughing.

"Sorry, have I been a bit tetchy? Tea with my blessing," he agreed. "Now come on, we can't do with you being late tonight."

Sister Morrell on the children's ward was small, fluffy haired and fragile. But she had an air of authority, a serenity in her blue eyes that Angela guessed would stand both patients and staff well in any crisis.

She introduced Angela to Michelle Walker, another auxiliary.

"Michelle will be off for the next three nights, but she'll show you the ropes. First I will take you round the wards, although your duties will be more or less in the kitchen for the time being."

There were four wards of six beds in the children's wing. Angela watched as Sister Marie Morrell eased an aching limb; put a supporting arm round small shoulders while they swallowed pills and medication; pulled tousled covers over sleeping children.

Lastly sister took her into a side ward. A young nurse, not much older than Angela, sat beside the bed where a small girl lay motionless.

Wires seemed to be attached to every part of her body, and the screen of a monitoring machine showed a pattern of lines that sister looked at closely.

Angela could not take her eyes from the bed. Long, fair hair fanned over the pillow, the child's cheeks were white, her eyes closed.

"She was in a car accident, but we'll pull her through," sister said softly as they left the room.

Angela's face was wet with tears, but Sister Marie shook her head.

"No tears, Angela. They are a luxury nurses cannot afford. They're no help to the patient, only to yourself. I understand you do hope to nurse, eventually?"

"Oh yes, Sister."

"Well, this will be a good grounding. I'll take you and leave you in Michelle's care now."

It was the early hours of the morning before Angela took her meal into the small room provided for them. Before she ate, she drew back part of the curtain and looked down on the sleeping town. The town she had grown up in, but had never seen as she saw it now.

Mostly it was in darkness, the street lights extinguished, but here and there a lighted window told of sleepless nights, perhaps illness, sorrow.

Angela felt very humble as she thought of her own inexperience, the way she had taken all life had to offer without giving in return.

She didn't pray. It was a long time since she had gone reluctantly to Sunday School, but from somewhere deep within rose an inner resolve, a resolution to give something back to the world, to justify her being.

★ ★ ★

On Sunday morning Paula heard her husband leave the house before she was up. She had hoped to see him before he left, but if he followed his usual pattern he would be home in the afternoon, after lunching at the golf club.

She ate a solitary breakfast, then, sure of her welcome, drove to Nesbit Street and was greeted by an excited Naomi.

"I'm going to see my daddy, I'm going to see my daddy!" She was singing the words over and over again.

"I can only sing low, because Angela's in bed. She's been up all night helping at the hospital. She doesn't go to the cafe any more." Naomi chatted as Paula brushed her hair. "Are you coming to see my daddy, Auntie Paula?"

"No love, I'll see him later. How pretty you look and how proud your father will be when he knows how you've coped."

"I wish Nan could come with us," Naomi said wistfully.

"I'll stay a bit with Nan when you've gone," Paula promised.

Mabel Nicholls hobbled to the front door to wave the car off, then Paula walked with her back to her room.

Mabel fidgeted a bit, then opened her bag.

"Mrs Firth, you're a business woman. I got this letter. What should I do?"

Paula read it in silence. Although nothing had been said she could guess the feeling of security, of independance retaining the tenancy of her own small home had given the old lady.

"They want me to sell," Mabel told her unnecessarily. "Says something about compulsory purchase if I don't agree. Can they do that?"

"Yes, I'm afraid they can. I think you should accept the offer, Nan," Paula said gently. "If they do force a sale you won't get as much for it, and you'd still lose the house."

She saw the way Mabel's eyes wandered round, and read her thoughts.

"Emma's a good woman, Mabel. You'll be all right here."

"Yes, I know that. It's just that, well — oh, never mind. I'm just being silly, sentimental. I'll put the money away for when my grandchildren need anything. It will be nice being able to help. I just wish Naomi was really ours. I shall miss her.

"In a funny way, she's helped me to settle here, made it bearable when I thought it never would be — "

"But you'll still see a lot of her — I'm sure of that. Naomi looks on you, on all this family as her own now."

"Yes, well — " Mabel put the letter away and clicked her bag shut. "That's enough of my whining. You've troubles of your own. How are things between you and that husband of yours?"

Paula smiled. She knew only too well that Mabel had never forgiven Hugh Firth for slapping Naomi.

"Not too good," she admitted. "I must go now, anyway. I need to do some straight talking. To sort my life out."

Mabel held out a hand.

"Thank you for talking to me, Paula, if you don't mind me calling you that. Think of yourself, remember we have only one life, and it is what we ourselves make of it that matters."

Paula felt quite calm as she parked her car behind her husband's in the wide drive. She went up to her room and renewed her make up, brushed her hair, and went downstairs with quiet determination in her eyes.

Hugh was in the drawing room, watching television, a whisky on the table beside him.

Paula crossed over and switched the set off.

"I need to talk," she told him.

"For heaven's sake, not just now," he grumbled.

"Would you prefer to hear what I have to say in the office tomorrow, then? I'm sure the staff would find it very interesting."

Hugh flushed uneasily.

"Very well, say what you have to and get it over."

"I want a divorce!"

"You want — like hell you do. You can forget that!"

"I want a divorce," Paula repeated, "and on my terms. You'd better listen. I've seen a flat I like, not too costly. I also want enough furniture from here to furnish it, and your shares in Siven's Office Equipment."

Hugh jumped up.

"You're mad, woman! You don't really think I'm going to buy you a flat and hand over my shares, just like that?"

"Just like that," Paula agreed. "After all you did say the business was running down, and I'm sure quite a few people, the police, and I suspect, the inland revenue among them, would be more than interested to know how the Office Reliant Company started. Not to mention where most of its stock comes from."

Hugh changed colour.

"Oh, yes. I know all about that. And I warn you if you don't agree I'll go through the usual channels and you'll lose a lot more than a few shares.

"I want your answer tonight," she told him. "I'll leave you to think it over."

11

"**D**ADDY! Daddy!" From the confines of his hospital bed David Bryant held his small daughter close.

Struggling to come to terms with the life that was now opening out in front of him, little Naomi represented a large part of the past he was trying so hard to bring into focus, and the future he was trying to find the courage to face.

He didn't say much, and his words of thanks to the two people who had helped his daughter through the last difficult weeks, were few, but sincere.

Emma and Bob Nicholls were content though, and asked few questions. David was still a shadow of his former self. There would be time for talk later. The main thing now was for him to get well enough to return home.

"Daddy, I don't want you to stay here. If you have to I want to stay as well."

"Sorry love, but you can't. I'll be home

soon. You heard the doctor say it might be Wednesday."

"But Gail's staying. Why can't I? I'll be good."

Naomi looked across to the half sister she had only just met, her eyes pleading for support.

Gail lifted Naomi down and took her to one side.

David watched as the older girl knelt and spoke earnestly to the eight-year-old. Already a deep affection had sprung up between the two and somewhere in his still uncertain mind, a sense of guilt mingled with other emotions.

He should have found Gail earlier. Naomi should not have had to grow up in ignorance of the fact that she had a sister, with only him to care for her. The two girls would have been good friends, Gail helping to take the place of the mother neither of them had known.

"I'll make it up somehow," he promised himself, fighting back the fatigue that was already troubling him. But Naomi was back.

"Gail and I have a secret," she announced, her eyes shining. "I'm going to help Auntie Emma get Bracken Heath ready, but there's something else as well. You will come home on Wednesday, won't you?"

"I'll try, love," he whispered. Then he reached into his locker and pulled out a picture. A cottage nestling in the lee of a bridge. The painting Ned had so carefully restored.

"Take this home for me, Naomi. It's very special. One day I'll tell you all about it."

David watched them go, his eyes already closing. But it was not yet time for sleep. The visit had pushed the door to the past a little further open.

"Don't force yourself to remember," the doctor had told him. But as he lay half awake, memories began to return.

The office, and the growing tension between him and his partner, Hugh Firth. His home, Bracken Heath, that had somehow never quite seemed like home after his wife, Catherine, died so soon after Naomi's birth.

When Gail looked at him he was asleep. She slipped on her jacket and went out for her evening meal at Sandra's cafe. Then, knowing David was all right she went for a walk round until it was time for her nightly call to Graham Stanley.

There was a lightness in Gail's step. A new feeling of belonging, of faith in the future in her heart. Her childhood in foster homes had been reasonably happy; but now, her love for Graham growing steadily stronger; and the knowledge that she had a family, that she was no longer alone in the world, gave her a new strength, a stake in the future and she knew she could look forward to a richer life than she had ever thought possible.

* * *

There were no welcoming fanfares when David walked into his home the following Wednesday. Only Emma and Naomi were there to greet him, just as they had always been.

Paula had elected to stay away, fearing that her presence might be regarded as an intrusion, and Bob Nicholls had gone to his work in the factory.

With great care Naomi carried a cup

of tea to her father, then scrambled on his knee, handing him a well thumbed exercise book.

"Look, I've written it all down for you. All about what I did when you weren't here. Gail thought about it and I've told you all sorts of things. That was my secret, so I had to come home and get it done."

David held her close.

"That's lovely, sweetheart. I shall love to read it. Now how about showing Gail her new home?"

So at last Emma was alone with him, and able to tell him how she had come to terms with his absence. She didn't give herself any praise, simply stated facts and told how everyone had pulled together.

But David knew who he had to thank for the way things had worked out for him, and as Emma left to make the meal, he was very thoughtful.

Meanwhile, Gail looked round the charming room Emma had prepared for her.

"You are going to live here?" Naomi asked anxiously. "Sisters always live together."

"Sorry, pet. I shall have to go home, back to Peebles, in a few days. I will come to stay with you again, but for now — "

Gail told Naomi about the art gallery and how Graham was looking after it for her.

"But your daddy will bring you to see me, and I'll paint a special picture, just for you."

★ ★ ★

During the next few days David Bryant improved by leaps and bounds. When Graham Stanley drove down at the weekend to take Gail home, he was almost his old self.

Then as it had been for many years, it was just the two of them. Emma spent the days at Bracken Heath, but, assured by the doctor that it would be all right, went home to sleep.

Naomi snuggled up to her father on the garden lounger.

"Tell me again about the gypsies, Daddy. Please?"

So David told her again how little

205

Rose, barely a year older than Naomi, had found him lying injured in the woods. How old Meg had taken care of him.

Naomi listened entranced as he went on to tell of life in the caravans, the meals cooked over open air fires, a way of life that sounded enchanting to the eight year old.

A few days later, Naomi asked her father to take her to see the gypsies.

"Please, Daddy? I want to see Rose and old Meg, and see in the caravan. Please?"

David looked doubtful. He knew how the gypsies guarded their privacy, but he saw the entreaty in Naomi's eyes, and promised to find out if there was any chance. He himself wanted to see them again. To thank them as best he could. Knowing how fierce their pride was, he knew it was only words they would accept.

★ ★ ★

It was just after lunch the following day when Paula called. David had not seen her since she visited him at the hospital, but he greeted her warmly, telling her he hoped to be fit for work, at least part time, very soon.

Paula shook her head. "There's no hurry.

"Naomi, I've just been to see Nan. She is missing you so much. How would you like to go to Nesbit Street and see them all again? I would take you and come to bring you home."

Naomi hesitated, glancing at her father. But David had sensed the underlying meaning behind Paula's suggestion, and nodded.

"Yes, I think you should. You could ask Laurie and Barry to come and spend a day with you."

So Naomi, armed with Nan's favourite chocolate biscuits, arrived again at Nesbit Street. It was hard to say who was most delighted, Naomi, Bob Nicholls, just home from work, or Mabel. The boys were out, off on some escapade of their own, so Naomi sat playing games with Mabel, until it was almost time to leave.

She gathered her things together, then

put her arms round Mabel, hugging her as the old lady had rarely been hugged before.

"Can I come and see you again, Nan?"

"As often as you like, love," Mabel assured her. "Now don't forget to say goodbye to Uncle Bob."

★ ★ ★

When she returned to Bracken Heath after taking Naomi to the Nicholls', Paula Firth sat opposite David Bryant and tried to find words for what she had to say.

"David, I know you won't be back at the office for a week or two, but I feel there is something I ought to tell you now. To give you a chance to think about it.

"Hugh is no longer to be a partner in the firm. We are getting a divorce and he is making his shares over to me."

David looked at her, stunned.

"But Paula, you and Hugh, you've been together so long."

"No, David. We haven't really been

together for a long time. Not as a husband and wife should be."

He stood up and took her hands.

"And me? What have I to think about?"

"I thought you might not like the idea of me taking more responsibility. After all, that wasn't what you agreed to in the first place."

"You know, Paula," he said slowly. "I think I will like that very much. My friendship with Hugh was only on the surface.

"But what about you? Are you still living with Hugh?"

Paula shook her head.

"No! I have a flat but it is being redecorated. At the moment I'm staying at a small hotel."

"Then move in here," David said eagerly. "There's plenty of room, and I'm sure it would be much more comfortable."

"Much more," Paula agreed with a smile. "But I don't think it would be a very good idea."

"You want more time to yourself, Emma told me the doctor said rest and quiet are essential. Naomi needs time to get adjusted, it hasn't been easy for her — "

She stopped, aware that David was looking at her with a deep intensity. She looked away, but he put a finger under her chin, tilting it so she had to look at him. "Paula, that day at the hospital. The first day when you came to see me — well, I thought I heard you say — "

Paula laid a finger on his lips.

"No, David. Let's just say we were all under stress, and it was a very emotional time. I — "

Her voice broke, and she lowered her eyes, afraid of what he might read there.

David Bryant looked at the woman he had worked with for so many years, and suddenly it was as though he was seeing her for the first time.

It was Paula who cut the moment short. Stepping back, she picked up her jacket, but before she left to collect Naomi, she turned to him.

"By the way, I couldn't help hearing Naomi asking you to take her to see the gypsies. It's only natural she wants to go after listening to all you've told her about them.

"If you decide to take her, and I'm certain they won't mind, I will run you down on Saturday. I know you haven't got a car yet, and in any case you're not fit to drive for a while longer."

So it was arranged, and on Saturday Paula drove round to Bracken Heath in good time.

Naomi chatted eagerly on the way to the camp; ate sausages and chips with relish when they stopped at a small roadside cafe and the two adults shared a smile. At least Naomi had recovered from any effect the events of the last few weeks had had on her.

When they drew up near the woods that sheltered the small gypsy camp from the open countryside, Paula stayed in the car.

"No," she answered when David urged her to accompany them. "I need some time to myself. I've brought flat shoes and some fruit. I'll pick you up about five."

She didn't say that her whole being felt bruised and shaken. To Hugh, she had appeared calm, almost uncaring; but once her whole life had revolved round Hugh Firth, and she had found making the final break, in such unpleasant circumstances, harrowing.

That it was the right thing to do, she was certain, but Hugh had not made it easy. So Paula found solace in the quiet of the countryside, which had played such a large part in her life before she had been caught up in Hugh's social whirl.

She knew that a few hours peace and solitude on the hills would ease her troubled mind more than any words could do.

David watched her drive away before taking his impatient daughter across the field to the camp.

The next few hours were pure enchantment for Naomi. Rose and she felt no strangeness, in spite of their different backgrounds. Rose was thrilled to find that Naomi could read and write, while Naomi listened with awe to the things Rose could tell her as they wandered into the woods.

As the children played, David sat with

old Meg on the steps of the van.

"I've a lot to thank you for, Meg," he told her, taking her work worn hand in his, and remembering how tenderly she had ministered to him as he lay almost senseless in her caravan.

"Nay, there's no need for thanks between friends," she answered. "You've a fine little lass there," she added.

So they talked for a while, then David, smiling, walked across to the cupboard and took out his old painting tray.

"Still there," he smiled.

"Aye! Well the boys don't have time for that in the summer. Have to get extra money earned before the winter, and it will soon be time for us to move on. They have a notion to let the younger ones have some schooling during the winter months."

David looked to where the two children were kneeling, deep in conversation.

"I think you should," he said quietly. "Young Rose will take to it like a duck to water. Anyway, let's go and look at my masterpiece."

So they wandered over to the partly restored, motorised van.

"My lads think I shall be in that this winter," old Meg told him. "But they're wrong. As long as my old Sam can keep going we'll travel together. I'll not wait around for someone to take me here and there. I've always wandered free and I'm too old to change my ways now."

David looked at the scorned van thoughtfully. He had spent so many hours on it, but there was still a lot to do.

Naomi was reluctant to leave. Rose was already laying the sticks to build a fire for the evening's cooking.

When the dark nights came the stoves in the vans would take the place of open fires, but on summer evenings most of the tribe liked to live by the old customs.

Naomi watched Rose, and begged her father to stay longer, but he was adamant.

"No, Naomi. Paula has a long drive home. You can see Rose again some other time."

But he was to find vague promises did not satisfy his daughter. A few mornings later she crept into his bed and put her arms round him.

"Daddy, I shall be nine soon. Do you know what I would like for my birthday?"

David, unprepared for what was to come, assured her he had no idea.

"A big party in the garden. With Rose and Old Meg and all the others. We could have fires and cook the food like the gypsies do — please Daddy? Please?"

David, knowing how rarely the Romanies varied from their usual haunts, tried to dissuade her, but finally promised to ask if it were possible. Besides, he had something he wanted to see Seth about.

His car was being replaced the next day. He would drive over and visit the camp on his own.

As it happened the small family band of gypsies had already planned to move to Yorkshire for the autumn, and at least part of the winter.

Old Meg had finally agreed with Seth that the children of school age should attend, at least part time. And they all honoured David as a good fellow, so Naomi got her birthday wish.

★ ★ ★

But before Naomi's birthday came, the motor van Meg had scorned arrived to take pride of place at the bottom of the garden.

Naomi was thrilled, but David waited until she was asleep before he rang Paula and asked her to come round.

"I've something to show you," he said, taking her hand.

"David! It's — it's magnificent," she breathed.

"I'll finish the outside and get Bob Nicholls working on the interior," he told her, turning her so she had to meet his eyes. "About a year's work I would say, give or take a month or two. Then holidays where the fancy takes — " he hesitated before his final word — "us."

His eyes, dark and serious, looked into hers. She smiled, a tremulous, rather uncertain smile, but she didn't look away.

"Give me time, David," she whispered.

He lifted her hand and pressed a kiss on the palm, folding her fingers over it.

"Hold on to that, and you can have

216

all the time you need. Just remember, I'm here, waiting."

★ ★ ★

The sun was shining and all was calm when Naomi woke on her ninth birthday morning. Soon the garden was a hive of activity as the men fixed fairy lights in the trees and lifted patches of turf where the fires would be lit. These were carefully rolled up and put out of harm's way to be relaid later.

Not only the garden, but the kitchen as well hummed with activity. Emma didn't trust open air cooking to feed her flock.

The big table groaned under the weight of extras Emma was cooking, 'just in case' and David, watching her quiet contentment as she worked, was reminded yet again how much he owed the Nicholls of Nesbit Street.

"Emma, is there anything you would like?" he asked. "Anything that would give you real pleasure?"

Emma laughed. "Not that I can think of. I've all I need, Mr Bryant. Bob now, well he did have a dream. He never mentions it now, but if he hadn't married me it would have come true by now."

"What would have come true?"

"His plans for a little workshop. Repairs and the like. Oh, he does some, from a garage, but — well, it isn't the same."

"Give me a little time, Emma, and we'll see what we can do between us."

"Oh, no! I wasn't meaning — "

"I know you weren't, but if that's what will make you happy, then that's what you shall have. Perhaps we could even manage a van, just a run-about, but road worthy."

Emma looked at him, unable to hide her surprise.

"He wouldn't let you down. He'd be a while before he could pay anything back — "

"There'll be no question of paying back. I don't think you realize how much I owe you, Emma Nicholls, and the rest of your family. If Naomi had been taken into care, handed over to strangers, this might not have had a happy ending."

"I only did what was right, and the lassie, well, she was a joy to us all.

Helped each one of us in her own way.

"Anyway," she said briskly, "that's enough talk for now. I've still the cake to finish. It's my present to Naomi."

When Emma looked at the completed cake, its nine candles ready to light, her thoughts went back to a young wife, sick and afraid in a hospital bed.

"Look after my baby, Emma," she had pleaded.

Emma knew she had done just that. Her promise had been kept.

Her thoughts were rudely interrupted by the arrival of her son, Laurie, staggering under the weight of a large, cumbersome, newspaper wrapped object.

Panting, he rested it on a chair, reddening as he met his mother's puzzled look.

"It's my present, for Naomi."

David, who had been enjoying a cup of tea and a surreptitious taste of Emma's baking, stepped forward.

"She's in the garden. Shall I help?"

"No thanks! I can manage."

Emma and David looked at each other as Laurie shouldered his mysterious parcel, and staggered into the garden.

Of one accord they crossed over and stood by the open window.

"It's for you, a birthday present," Laurie told Naomi. Both children proceeded to tear off the paper.

"It's Dad's materials, but I made it when he wasn't there. Sorry the paper's stuck. I only painted it yesterday. It will wash off when it rains. This was the only colour I could find."

"It's a bird table," he explained, as Naomi continued to stare in silence.

"It's lovely!" she gasped. "I always wanted one, but will it stand up?"

"Of course it will!"

Laurie released his hold and the construction wobbled precariously.

"Well, it did in the garage. It must be the ground that isn't level."

"We can prop it up," suggested Naomi. "Near the arch. We don't want it to fall over with the birds on."

David and Emma smothered their giggles as the two children wedged the bright blue object into place. By this time Rose had joined them, and some of the other adults were trying to hide their smiles.

"Hold it while I get some stones," Laurie commanded. Meekly Naomi and Rose obeyed.

Then they stepped back and surveyed their handiwork. Naomi reached up and planted a kiss on the cheek of the embarrassed donor.

"Thanks, Laurie, it's a lovely present. Come on, let's go and ask Emma for some crumbs."

★ ★ ★

Later, as they sat round the glowing fire, where, in spite of the empty pots the delicious aroma of outdoor cooking still lingered, David Bryant looked across at the lined face of old Meg.

In the morning, these people who had so strangely become his friends, would be moving on. David knew he would not see them again.

In spite of his growing confidence in the future, the thought saddened him.

Naomi felt she would burst with happiness. All the people she cared about were there. Her father, sharing the same bale of hay, had his arm round her.

221

Gail sat next to them, Graham Stanley by her side.

Gail and Naomi had another secret. Soon, perhaps next year, she, Naomi, would be a bridesmaid. Gail would take her and let her choose her own dress. It was lovely having a sister.

Angela Nicholls was near her mother and Paula Firth. Naomi saw Angela slip her hand into that of Colin Ankers. Bob Nicholls was carefully raking hot ashes together. Barry walked from the kitchen with yet another plate of food, carefully avoiding his mother's eagle eye. Naomi thought about her presents. The film in the camera her father had given her was already nearly used. A real grown up box of chocolates from Jeremy, who was away making arrangements for his new college course.

Then there was the writing set from Angela. Nan had decided on a pretty, lined sewing box, and Naomi loved it. Nan had even come to the party. Naomi smiled across at her as she sat in her wheel chair, cosily wrapped against any chill from the night air.

Rose had given her a basket of dried

flowers, all her own work and Naomi told her that was far better than being able to read. But Rose was going to go to school, and when she could read and write, she had promised Naomi a letter.

There were carved animals from the other Romanies, and a small, ash plant walking stick from old Meg.

She smiled at Laurie as he walked across to her, holding out a napkin.

"Some hot chestnuts," he told her. "I peeled them for you."

"Thanks, I love them."

"I know. You always ate most when Mum boiled them. These are even nicer."

The night was calm, still. Slowly the gypsies began to sing, gypsy songs and old favourites their hosts could join in.

Mabel Nicholls, watching the child she had grown to love and her grandson, as they sat together, felt a warmth in her heart. To her, Naomi was already part of the Nicholls of Nesbit Street. Perhaps one day —

THE WILDERNESS WALK
Sheila Bishop

Stifling unpleasant memories of a misbegotten romance in Cleave with Lord Francis Aubrey, Lavinia goes on holiday there with her sister. The two women are thrust into a romantic intrigue involving none other than Lord Francis.

THE RELUCTANT GUEST
Rosalind Brett

Ann Calvert went to spend a month on a South African farm with Theo Borland and his sister. They both proved to be different from her first idea of them, and there was Storr Peterson — the most disturbing man she had ever met.

ONE ENCHANTED SUMMER
Anne Tedlock Brooks

A tale of mystery and romance and a girl who found both during one enchanted summer.

CLOUD OVER MALVERTON
Nancy Buckingham

Dulcie soon realises that something is seriously wrong at Malverton, and when violence strikes she is horrified to find herself under suspicion of murder.

AFTER THOUGHTS
Max Bygraves

The Cockney entertainer tells stories of his East End childhood, of his RAF days, and his post-war showbusiness successes and friendships with fellow comedians.

MOONLIGHT
AND MARCH ROSES
D. Y. Cameron

Lynn's search to trace a missing girl takes her to Spain, where she meets Clive Hendon. While untangling the situation, she untangles her emotions and decides on her own future.

NURSE ALICE IN LOVE
Theresa Charles

Accepting the post of nurse to little Fernie Sherrod, Alice Everton could not guess at the romance, suspense and danger which lay ahead at the Sherrod's isolated estate.

POIROT INVESTIGATES
Agatha Christie

Two things bind these eleven stories together — the brilliance and uncanny skill of the diminutive Belgian detective, and the stupidity of his Watson-like partner, Captain Hastings.

LET LOOSE THE TIGERS
Josephine Cox

Queenie promised to find the long-lost son of the frail, elderly murderess, Hannah Jason. But her enquiries threatened to unlock the cage where crucial secrets had long been held captive.

THE TWILIGHT MAN
Frank Gruber

Jim Rand lives alone in the California desert awaiting death. Into his hermit existence comes a teenage girl who blows both his past and his brief future wide open.

DOG IN THE DARK
Gerald Hammond

Jim Cunningham breeds and trains gun dogs, and his antagonism towards the devotees of show spaniels earns him many enemies. So when one of them is found murdered, the police are on his doorstep within hours.

THE RED KNIGHT
Geoffrey Moxon

When he finds himself a pawn on the chessboard of international espionage with his family in constant danger, Guy Trent becomes embroiled in moves and countermoves which may mean life or death for Western scientists.

TIGER TIGER
Frank Ryan

A young man involved in drugs is found murdered. This is the first event which will draw Detective Inspector Sandy Woodings into a whirlpool of murder and deceit.

CAROLINE MINUSCULE
Andrew Taylor

Caroline Minuscule, a medieval script, is the first clue to the whereabouts of a cache of diamonds. The search becomes a deadly kind of fairy story in which several murders have an other-worldly quality.

LONG CHAIN OF DEATH
Sarah Wolf

During the Second World War four American teenagers from the same town join the Army together. Forty-two years later, the son of one of the soldiers realises that someone is systematically wiping out the families of the four men.

THE LISTERDALE MYSTERY
Agatha Christie

Twelve short stories ranging from the light-hearted to the macabre, diverse mysteries ingeniously and plausibly contrived and convincingly unravelled.

TO BE LOVED
Lynne Collins

Andrew married the woman he had always loved despite the knowledge that Sarah married him for reasons of her own. So much heartache could have been avoided if only he had known how vital it was to be loved.

ACCUSED NURSE
Jane Converse

Paula found herself accused of a crime which could cost her her job, her nurse's reputation, and even the man she loved, unless the truth came to light.

CHATEAU OF FLOWERS
Margaret Rome

Alain, Comte de Treville needed a wife to look after him, and Fleur went into marriage on a business basis only, hoping that eventually he would come to trust and care for her.

CRISS-CROSS
Alan Scholefield

As her ex-husband had succeeded in kidnapping their young daughter once, Jane was determined to take her safely back to England. But all too soon Jane is caught up in a new web of intrigue.

DEAD BY MORNING
Dorothy Simpson

Leo Martindale's body was discovered outside the gates of his ancestral home. Is it, as Inspector Thanet begins to suspect, murder?

A GREAT DELIVERANCE
Elizabeth George

Into the web of old houses and secrets of Keldale Valley comes Scotland Yard Inspector Thomas Lynley and his assistant to solve a particularly savage murder.

'E' IS FOR EVIDENCE
Sue Grafton

Kinsey Millhone was bogged down on a warehouse fire claim. It came as something of a shock when she was accused of being on the take. She'd been set up. Now she had a new client — herself.

A FAMILY OUTING IN AFRICA
Charles Hampton and Janie Hampton

A tale of a young family's journey through Central Africa by bus, train, river boat, lorry, wooden bicycle and foot.

THE PLEASURES OF AGE
Robert Morley

The author, British stage and screen star, now eighty, is enjoying the pleasures of age. He has drawn on his experiences to write this witty, entertaining and informative book.

THE VINEGAR SEED
Maureen Peters

The first book in a trilogy which follows the exploits of two sisters who leave Ireland in 1861 to seek their fortune in England.

A VERY PAROCHIAL MURDER
John Wainwright

A mugging in the genteel seaside town turned to murder when the victim died. Then the body of a young tearaway is washed ashore and Detective Inspector Lyle is determined that a second killing will not go unpunished.

DEATH ON A HOT SUMMER NIGHT
Anne Infante

Micky Douglas is either accident-prone or someone is trying to kill him. He finds himself caught in a desperate race to save his ex-wife and others from a ruthless gang.

HOLD DOWN A SHADOW
Geoffrey Jenkins

Maluti Rider, with the help of four of the world's most wanted men, is determined to destroy the Katse Dam and release a killer flood.

THAT NICE MISS SMITH
Nigel Morland

A reconstruction and reassessment of the trial in 1857 of Madeleine Smith, who was acquitted by a verdict of Not Proven of poisoning her lover, Emile L'Angelier.

POM

Library at Home Service
Community Services
Hounslow Library, CentreSpace
24 Treaty Centre, High Street
Hounslow TW3 1ES

YOUR COMMUNITY
YOUR SERVICES

0	1	2	3	4	5	6	7	8	9
3480	1151	532		944	715	116	3087	818	
9810	991	902		704	525	6706	121	728 3218	
7920	861	212	943			6309 706	2	7968	
								7828	
					30788			3308	
							3407	3488	
						346			

P10-L-2061